VOW TO THE KING

A DARK MAFIA ROMANCE

SHANNA HANDEL

For V. C. Andrews who got me hooked on dark romance.

WELCOME

Vow to the King: A Dark Mafia Romance

Shanna Handel

Copyright © 2022 Shanna Handel

Credits to my wonderful team:

Artwork by Pop Kitty Design

Photography by

WANDER AGUIAR PHOTOGRAPHY LLC

Editing by Jane Beyer

Proofread by Julie Barney

ARC Director Jess Bracewell

Welcome to the story...

The king of the mafia swore off love. Then he met... *her.*

Emilia

It starts as an interview.

The mafia king needs brides for his brothers.

An arranged marriage to bind our families.

He sees the bruises I wear.

He wants to protect me.

He demands to be obeyed.

He steals me from my home.

I fight back.

But when he puts his hands on me...

I find my resistance is futile.

Each time I push him away, it's with weaker hands.

He took my innocence, but I can't let him take...

My heart.

Liam

She's a tiny thing, so young and naïve.

Beautiful and brave but loyal to a fault.

She needs the firm hand of a strong man.

Just... not my own.

She was meant to marry one of my brothers.

I never wanted a ring on my own finger.

But now I want to put my hands on her.

Tear her innocence away from her.

Be the first and the only man to touch her.

I can't get her out of my mind.

I've gone from wanting to punish her...

To wanting to make her mine.

Forever.

SHANNA HANDEL

E *milia*

TONIGHT IS *THAT* NIGHT IN MY HOUSE. THE ONE TERRIBLE NIGHT OF the year that the men in my family lock themselves in my father's study and drink too much whiskey, thereby avoiding their emotions. Not that the other nights around here are great or anything. This one is just particularly disturbing.

It's the anniversary of my mother's death.

They won't talk about their feelings or admit they miss her. Instead, they pour one another deep, cut-crystal tumblers of the amber liquor. I, on the other hand, do my best to avoid them. I choose to cry my eyes out alone, hiding in the library, my face buried in one of the last few things I own of my mother's. Her books. They're the only things of hers my father didn't remove from this house in his attempt to scrub the place of her memory when she died.

These aren't *quite* all of her books. One rainy afternoon I was exploring our dusty old attic and I found a bunch of paperbacks hidden in a corner behind an old chair, stacked neatly in brown paper grocery bags. Pages and pages of dark romance, the women falling for men with harsh hands and handsome faces. Those books found a new hiding place.

Under my bed.

Holding my mother's leather-bound book in my hands makes me ache for her.

A single tear trails down my cheek, falling from my chin and dampening the page. My brothers hate when I cry. They see it as a woman's weakness, to shed tears. They like to punish me when they find me crying.

My heart falls as I hear heavy footsteps headed right to me. Ignoring the closed door, Antonio, my oldest and most vicious brother, disturbs my peace. With bold green eyes, straight dark hair down to his shoulders, and high cheekbones, he'd almost be handsome if his heart weren't so charred. He throws open the heavy door.

The hard look on his angled face berates me before he even opens his mouth. His green eyes glitter with meanness. "Ah, the little bird is reading."

I'm slight but strong and he calls me little bird. It's his joke about me being small and held in this cage that is our crumbling mansion.

"You know I hate when you call me that." I dip my nose deeper in my book. "Please, go away."

He rips the book out of my hands.

My chest tightens at the sight of him holding such a precious belonging. Antonio has a habit of destroying beautiful things.

"Don't!" I grab for it, terrified he'll toss it in the fire.

He holds it just out of my reach, a cruel smile curling at the corners of his tormenting lips. He tosses it to the floor. It flutters open, landing facedown. I scoop the book up, grateful it's safe in my hands and not in the fireplace.

"There's a special place in hell for people who disrespect books like you do." I smooth the pages, close it gently, and lay the leather-bound book on the table beside my wingback chair.

My brother moves in close. Too close. I can feel heat and anger coming off him. The scent of whiskey pours from his mouth.

The tips of his fingers dig into my skin as he pulls me from my chair. I try to pull myself from his grasp but he's too strong.

He grips my upper arm, holding it tight. "You need to get over her."

"I'm fine. I was just reading, minding my own business—"

"No," he sneers. "You were crying."

"Get over her? Is that what you're doing with all that whiskey? Forgetting her?" I stare at Antonio, remembering when we were kids how he begged my mother to tell him stories about her child-hood, growing up in the countryside. "Why do you all drink your-selves silly on this night, then? Is it random, or are you hurting too?"

My words anger him. How dare I suggest that he, too, is weak in the absence of our mother. I see venom rising in his face. Fury flashes in his gaze.

"Shut up." He gives me a hard shove, his hand returning between my shoulder blades as he pushes me out of the library. "And go to bed. You don't need to be down here."

"Fine. I'm going. Enjoy your poison." I move toward the stairs.

He watches me briefly to be sure I obey. I turn my face away, grabbing the smooth banister. I release a deep breath when he finally leaves me, turning down the hall to rejoin our brothers.

The door to my father's study closes, the lock clicking behind him. Deep voices rumble down the long, dark hall. Funny. Usually when they drink, they get loud, laughing or fighting. Tonight, their tones are dull, serious. What are they discussing? Leaving the stairs, I creep down the hall, pressing an ear against the wood.

My heart hammers against my ribcage, fearful of what Antonio will do to me if he catches me. I focus on their voices, but I can't make out the words. Maybe the surname Bachman? They're another mafia family, more powerful than mine, that recently moved to the lakefront.

The men are talking so low, I can't be sure that's what I heard. The only sound I hear clearly is the blood whooshing past my eardrum. They're up to no good, I'm sure.

Hate and nerves prick at my skin, making me uneasy. I need to get out of this prison. I need to feel the night air on my skin, release some endorphins. I need a run. Time for this little bird to fly from her cage.

I'm wearing biker shorts and a cropped tee from my earlier bodyweight workout in the garden. I just need to grab my shoes, and I'll be gone. I'm experienced at going unnoticed.

Leaving the door to my father's study, I tiptoe toward the massive foyer. My worn sneakers sit ready by the front door. I slip them on. I grab the ornate metal doorknob, its carvings cold in my hand. The door creaks as I open it.

I flinch, squeezing my eyes shut tight and freezing in place like a little kid. If I don't move, they can't see me.

No one comes.

I glide through the door, pulling it softly closed behind me.

Please let them all be passed out by the time I get home.

The cool night air wakes up my skin as I jog down the gravel drive, pebbles and stones crunching beneath the thin soles of my shoes. Picking up speed, I run through the tall iron gates they've left open. I make it to the paved road, the feeling of my long ponytail swishing behind me, swinging like a pendulum as my feet hit the road, one after the other. It's a steady rhythm and it lulls me into a sense of peace, even though my life feels anything but peaceful.

The moon is almost full, and it lights my way, casting a blue glow against the dark pavement. It's my own world. There's no one out here but me. I push myself a little harder, chasing those endorphins I'm lusting after. I love a good runner's high. My family keeps me locked away from the world. Working out is my only joy.

I'm so lost in keeping my pace, it's not till the car is right behind me that I hear it.

My impulsive decision to take this run settles heavy in my stomach. Out by myself on the road at night. Not smart. Who's out this late? Very few people use this road. We live deep in the forest, hundreds of untouched acres in our name. Ours is the only house for miles. The road leads to the lake, to the gorgeous estates that dot the shore.

Please pass me. My skin crawls as the car slows.

It pulls up to my side, keeping time with me. I try to pretend it's not there. Ignore it and it'll go away. I peek at it out of the corner of my eye. A black SUV with dark, tinted windows.

Staring straight ahead, I keep running.

I don't know what else to do.

Please don't let it be men sent by my father. I'd been so quiet. The study door was closed. They were all drunk and engaged in whatever they were talking about. Surely, they didn't hear me leave.

There's the whirr of the motor of a window rolling down. My body goes tight, as rigid as a wire drawn taut from two ends. I keep running.

A low voice comes to me, rumbling through the night. "Little girls should be safe at home. Don't you know the kinds of men that prowl through these woods?"

Ice flows down my spine.

"Yes," I say, keeping my eyes forward and my voice steady. No one knows I'm gone from home, but this man doesn't know that. "My brothers prowl these woods. They're terrifying."

I keep my pace, one foot in front of the other, trying to ignore the hammering of my heart he caused. I can feel his eyes heavy on my body as I move.

To my horror, the SUV pulls to a stop.

There is no other choice. I take off. My legs burst into an all-out sprint. I listen for footsteps, but the only sound is my feet slapping against the pavement. I don't look back, pulling heavy breaths into my burning lungs.

Hairs stand on the back of my neck, perspiration prickles at my underarms. How many times has my father warned me not to come out here? How many enemies has he warned me of, telling me they'd love nothing more than to deflower the Accardi princess?

Now the footsteps come, heavy with determination.

I glance at the thick, dark woods to my left. They're my only hope. I can't afford a backward glance over my shoulder to see if he's gaining on me. I dart off the road, my feet hitting the soft earth.

Strong forearms dig into my belly, knocking the wind from me. No! My assailant holds me tighter, my back pressing into his chest. I can feel the muscles beneath his shirt shifting.

His arms lock around me, creating a prison around my ribcage.

"What do you want?" I hiss, grabbing at his arms, trying to push them away.

His mouth finds my ear, his breath hot against my cheek, and it tickles my skin, making the bits of hair that loosened from my ponytail flutter. "To teach you a lesson."

It's the same deep voice that reprimanded me from the SUV.

His hard palm runs over my trembling midriff. My cropped shirt rises, his hot skin caressing my cold torso. My muscles constrict, my belly going hard as a rock. Fear and remorse fill me.

What have I gotten myself into? What is he going to do to me?

One big hand presses into my belly, holding me against him, pushing my ass against the tops of his hard thighs. I dig my fingers into his forearm, a feeble attempt to dislodge him.

Heat from his body travels through his clothing, warming my skin. The clean scent of him hits me, cedar and man. This is the closest to a stranger I've ever been. My mind goes to my mother's other collection of books, the ones that hide under my bed. The spicy romance novels that I've dog-eared, re-reading my favorite scenes time and time again.

Is it the cool night air or the feel of his body that has my breasts heavy, my nipples tightening against my sports bra? A shiver tears through me, making me shudder and as I do, my hips roll, my ass accidently circling his lap.

Who *am* I, responding like this? I'm acting like one of the women in my books, wanting this and fearful of it all at the same time. My body is at war with my mind.

He lets out a low groan. The hand on my breast becomes his pinning hand, the one on my belly changing position, sliding up around my neck. He holds it lightly in his hand, his mouth so close to my ear now, his lips are touching my skin.

"What," I say again, my voice shaking, "do you want?"

"I told you." He drags his hand upward, smoothing over my curves, the pad of his thumb brushing ever so slightly over my traitorous nipple. "I want to teach you a lesson."

"I'm all good on lessons, thanks." Why is my ass pushing harder against him? My hips moving with a mind of their own... What is wrong with me?

"There are bad, bad men out here. Men that would take an innocent little girl like you and destroy her." He cups my breast in his palm, squeezing. "Let me tell you what you're going to do now..."

Is he one of the men my father warned me about...?

The idea and his touch cause my body to go to war with itself. Fear and adrenaline unite, wrapping around my spine. At the same time, dampness creeps between my thighs.

He continues, breath hot on my skin. "You're going to turn around and run home. We'll follow you in our car to be sure you get home safely. And don't let me find you out here again." His hand moves from my breast, slowly palming my belly, my hip.

He turns me slightly and snakes his arm around my waist, grabbing half my ass in his hand. A gasp, sharp and shocked, comes from me as he clutches my curves, the tips of his fingers pressing into my crack, one wandering middle finger pressing hard against my rear entrance.

This stranger has his finger pressing into my asshole...

His intrusion makes me shoot up on the balls of my feet, my fingers clutching at the forearm of the hand that holds my neck. His touch becomes more aggressive, his finger pushing harder through the spandex of my shorts.

I can't breathe. I can't think.

His words tear me from my cloud of shock. "I don't ever want you on this road alone again. Do you understand?" His finger pushes harder through my clothing. The unspoken threat of where he'd punish me if he found me out here again hangs between us in the air, heavy and cold as a block of ice.

His fingers tighten around my nipple till I squeal. "If you understand, say 'yes, sir.'"

Should I try to kick him, stomp on his foot, run away? I look to the SUV. The door in the back is open. He has a driver, so at least one other man is with him.

What can I do other than obey?

I force the shameful words from my mouth. "Yes, sir."

He gives another groan like when my ass rubbed against him. He likes that. When I call him sir, when I obey.

"Now run home to daddy and tell him what you've done."

"Like hell I'll do that. I'd like to live to see another day."

His response is a dark, rumbling laugh, one I feel against my back.

His hands move to my shoulders, turning me to face him. My gaze flits up to his. Eyes so dark they glitter like cut onyx. Dark, wavy hair. Olive skin. A short, well-trimmed beard, lighter than his hair.

A face too handsome to be forgotten.

"I'm going. Now," I say.

"Good choice," he says, another laugh echoing in his chest.

I take off running, my feet moving as fast as the beats of my heart. I hear the car door close behind me and for the entire quarter-mile run home, I'm terrified that the car will stop again.

That he'll change his mind and climb down from that big SUV and...

I reach the gravel drive, sneakers crunching against stone. The car stays on the road. I can't see inside the tinted windows, but I know he's watching me all the way to the front door of my house.

As soon as I open it, a slice of dim light from inside creeping over the porch, the car pulls away.

I'm left alone with my hammering heart, its beat pulsating all the way down to my melting core.

I close the door, pausing only a moment to lean my head against it and breathe.

Shaking, I slip off my shoes, the rubber of the toe pulling away from the fabric, then set them neatly where they were before I left.

Alone in my room, I take a long, lukewarm shower in my tiny ensuite bathroom, wishing our old hot water heater could keep up. My calves ache. I press my palms against the chipped tiles of the shower, stretching my legs and feet out behind me to relieve the pain.

I dress in sweats and a tee, sit on my bed, and dry my hair as best I can with a towel. I stare out the window, over the small balcony off my room, taking in the huge moon that looms over this night.

The very moon that witnessed what happened to me on the road.

What's this?

A small, blinking red light catches my eye as it floats toward the balcony. I move closer to the window, picking up the whirring sound of a small motor or something. I open the balcony door, a cool breeze chilling my freshly showered skin.

A white and black machine flies my way. A drone, I think? I've seen my brothers and their friends messing around with one, a light, plastic model, taking turns flying it in the backyard with a controller.

This one looks more heavy-duty, expensive, as it moves closer and I get a better look. A white parcel hangs down from it, tied by thin ropes. Who's flying it? I move out onto the balcony, looking down. There's no one in sight.

I stand in the center of the moonlit balcony, my wet hair lying down my back, the towel draped over my shoulder. The drone hovers above my head, just out of reach. There's a small, steel claw holding the twine. The claw opens, releasing the ropes. The box drops.

My arms fly out, catching the box as it falls. It's fairly light in my arms. What could it hold? I stare down at the lid. There's a note attached. Should I open it?

Curiosity wins out over safety concerns, and I pull back the lid. Nestled in the white paper is a gorgeous pair of pink and gray Brooks Aurora running shoes, something I could never dream of owning. I check the tag beneath the tongue. Six and a half. They're my size.

They can only be from one person. The man on the road. But I've only been home, what? An hour? How could he pull this off? He's got to be crazy rich with a team of minions at his disposal.

I slide a nail under the edge of the envelope, pulling the creamy cardstock from it.

NEXT TIME KEEP YOUR RUNS AT THE GYM, LITTLE GIRL. THERE ARE *wolves in these woods.*

Liam Bachman

2

L *iam*

IN THE ORDINARY WORLD, THE IDEA OF MARRIAGE WOULD BRING UP choices. A person chooses whether to marry in the first place, and if so, to whom. In our world, there are other decisions that need to be made, carefully weighed against each outcome, like the sliding of chess pieces. Cause and effect. Orders given, required to be obeyed.

There are few choices.

I make the decisions and I've decided it's time. It's time for my four younger brothers to marry, to settle down. They joined the Bachman Brotherhood with me, followed me here to Italy to establish our estate, The Villa, to aid me in making our stand, expanding our mafia in Italy. They'd follow me to the ends of the Earth and that includes walking down the aisle if I say so.

My brothers, Cannon, Tristan, Hunter, and Dom – short for Dominick, the only one in the family with a name that fits in around here – are homegrown, all-American boys who've taken Italy by storm. Women in this country fall all over themselves for my boys. Ladies bump into my brothers in town and they flirt, teasing them about their American accents. They troll around our part of the lake, laying out topless on their boats, watching my shirtless brothers toss a football on the shore of the lake.

And my brothers are never rude. They pay the ladies just as much attention back. The front door of The Villa ought to be one of those automatic rotating ones with the stream of women coming and going.

Cannon, aptly and presciently named by my mother given the way he constantly fires off his unfiltered thoughts, is the only one not bringing girls around The Villa. That's because the man owns our family's kink club, Fire, a gorgeous, gated estate about a ten-minute drive from my place, where he has a guesthouse of his own.

Yes, it's time they married.

And each marriage will be carefully arranged to keep the Bachman family name in its strongest position, woven together with other powerful families through purchased vows.

Today, I begin my interviews.

I will remain single. I don't have the time or desire to be tied to one woman. I like my female companionship the way I like my occasional espresso drinks. Steaming hot but quickly done with, void of emotions, leaving me with a charge of energy for the rest of the day.

I don't do the dating stuff.

They call it "falling" in love for a reason. You lose control. And only a fool would choose to jump off a cliff.

There is one woman who calls to me, and I've gone to her more than a handful of times. Widow Russo, who lives in a French-style chalet across the lake. Things remain casual between us, but we know what we're doing and appreciate one another's talents.

Mid-forties, she's got about a decade on me. She knows how to please a man and more importantly, herself. Finally over the grief she felt from her husband's death, she's found happiness in herself. She's not looking to remarry and enjoys talking business.

I'm seeing the Widow Russo after this. I remind myself not to rush the upcoming interview. I look down at my notes.

My first potential bride-to-be is from a family whose land borders ours, their dilapidated estate nestled in the dark woods. A family with a strong Italian name, strong alliances, feared in this area. Our American Bachman Brotherhood needs to have local allies like them as we expand our mafia across Italy.

What the Accardis lack in fortune, they make up for with a violent thirst for blood. I have plenty of wealth to go around; what I need are henchmen. The Accardi clan would be a perfect solution. A slew of brothers as strong and cunning as my own, but their fall into poverty has made them desperate to rise to the top once more.

Desperation can make a powerful ally or an unpredictable enemy.

If the Accardis bleed financially much longer, they'll soon lose men. They want this marriage.

Badly.

I'm ready to get started. I look to Andre, standing guard by the tall, heavy door of my office. "Bring her to me."

A waif of a girl comes fluttering in behind my guard. Dressed in a black sleeveless dress with her dark blonde hair done up, styled to add years to her age. It doesn't work. Her bare face is so innocent, so fresh, she barely looks her age of twenty.

I think of Widow Russo and the self-assurance she carries in her shoulders. Mature. Beautiful. Wise. She's the type I usually go for.

I like my women to be just that, women. Not girls.

So why did I chase this girl down on the road last night? Put my hands on her and warn her? It was a fluke. I blame it on the moon. She must have cast a spell on me.

I almost write her off, ready to pen down in my notes *not strong enough for our lifestyle,* but then her gray-green eyes find mine. I remember her body against mine on the road. So responsive to my hold. Her gaze once again surprises me with its strength and fire. Her pretty pout is set in a steely bloom. She stands silent, waiting for me to speak.

Maybe...

Let's see what she has to say for herself.

"Emilia Accardi," I say. Her surname means hearty and brave. Standing at about five foot three and a hundred and ten pounds soaking wet but with her gaze steady on mine, she's only one of those things. "Has your family made you aware of our offer?"

"Yes."

"Good." I scan down the paper, moving on with my questions.

"I've been raised knowing that I would be married off for my family's benefit. I just didn't realize it would be to this family. A family where it's okay to just accost a girl on the road?"

Her tight voice drags my eyes back up to her. "I merely issued a friendly warning. I was trying to help my neighbor, your father, look out for you."

"Well. You treated me like..." Her face betrays her for a moment, showing her shame, but she straightens her spine and cocks her hip. "Like one of your animals, needing to be trained. You've made an offer to purchase me. You want to buy me like I'm a car. Or a pet. A horse to add to your stables."

I hold back a laugh. "A pet? Not quite. The Bachman family isn't in the business of buying people. We simply want to make an alliance with your family. We need to earn the trust of the locals and aligning with your father does that. We're building an empire. Would you like to be a part of that?"

Ignoring my question, she crosses her thin but surprisingly toned arms over her chest.

She asks a question of her own. "Is there going to be an exchange of money when you make this alliance?"

"Of course." I nod. "Nothing gets done in our world without the exchange of blood or money. I've offered each potential bride's father a generous dowry to buy their allegiance."

"Then you're buying me." She raises a perfectly arched brow, a few shades darker than her light hair, right at me.

I tap my pen against the paper, wondering which of my two columns this girl will end up in. *Yes* or *No*. I decide to drop the act and meet her where she is. I respect her bluntness.

Forgetting my notes, I lean back in my chair, folding my fingers into a pyramid beneath my chin and take her in for a moment.

She's slight but seems strong. Young and perhaps foolish, but brave.

"Fine," I say. "Yes. We've put in a generous offer to purchase your hand in marriage. I'd be giving your father money that your family desperately needs, to arrange your marriage to one of my brothers, thus uniting our families. What do you think?"

"I think it's archaic." With agitation, she taps the toe of a ballet-slippered foot against my polished hardwood floor. "Just like everything else in our world. Buying and selling women to create a false sense of comradery that—let's be honest—disappears in a year, when one of my father's hotheaded captains pops a cap in one of your guys over a deal not split exactly 50/50, and the ties you've tried so hard to bind dissolve in a split-second, and the families are at war."

I shrug. "It's quite possible."

"Then why bother?"

"Because this is the way things are done."

"Well, maybe it's time to do things a new way."

Her tongue is sharp. She's bright. Might be a match for Dom who, despite his name, is the most laid-back member of our family. This girl could bring him some fire.

Everything about her pleases me.

I pick up my pen, move it to the *Yes* column, and scratch her name onto the paper. *Emilia Accardi.*

I nod to Andre who waits for my command. "You can go."

She gives me a curious parting glance. She turns toward the door, keeping her head held high as she readies to make her exit.

But as she turns to leave, I see something I don't like.

"Wait."

Four fingertip-shaped bruises dance in a line down her upper arm. Fresh and angry and purple. A clear mark of someone who grabbed her in anger. I didn't see these bruises on the road last night, as her upper arms were covered by the sleeves of her T-shirt.

"Who hurt you?" I ask.

She follows my gaze to her arm, sliding a hand up to cover it. She looks away. "No one."

"One of your brothers?" I've heard stories of the vicious Accardi brood and how they put their hands on things that they shouldn't.

Mainly women. I didn't know their proclivities extended to their own flesh and blood.

She says nothing.

I ask again. "Do your brothers hurt you?"

"No." Her eyes are stone but her bottom lip quivers as she lies.

She's loyal, this one. I value that. Only she's loyal to the wrong men. That will soon change.

"The truth," I say, my tone harsh enough to make her reconsider her stance.

She eyes me a moment and what she sees in me makes her cave.

She shrugs. "No more than I hurt them. I fight back. You should know that about me. If you're going to make a purchase." She narrows her gaze as if inviting me into the ring.

I could pin her slight figure to my dark wood wall with one finger.

I hold back a laugh. She's serious and so to laugh at her would offend. I detest rudeness.

But these half-moons on her arm complicate things. Knowing what I know now, I won't send her back home.

She'll have to stay here till I decide what to do with her.

"Andre," I say. "Take Emilia to see Marta."

He nods. "Yes, sir."

I watch her leave, more closely than a prospective brother-in-law should. As I give her a longer look, I see the shapeless form of her dress is hiding firm curves beneath it. Her calves are toned from her midnight runs.

She's young and small and cold, but inside she's burning bright with fire.

EMILIA

HE KNOWS IT WAS ME, THE GIRL HE ACCOSTED ON THE ROAD. I SAW the flash of recognition in his eyes the moment I walked in the room. Was his bringing me here today merely a coincidence, or did he want to torture me further?

I've always known I would marry to help my family. But does it have to be to this family? I've heard rumors of their controlling ways with women, then last night, experienced them firsthand. Standing there in his office, I couldn't help but stand up for myself.

I know how our world works. I just didn't want to let him off the hook that easy without pushing back a little.

Such a monster. Touching me last night in such intimate ways then this morning acting like he'd never met me. Now, locking me in his pretty rooms under the guise of trying to keep me safe?

No, thank you to him on all counts.

I think of him on the road, grazing and squeezing my breast, his breath hot in my ear. A wave of hatred and warmth flows through me. I've been locked away in my room reading too many spicy romance novels. My choice in books has tricked my body into thinking this is normal, making desire rise in me at the thought of his hands on my body.

I must get back to my family. Yes, they're brutes. Yes, they put their hands where they shouldn't, but so does he.

He's the one I need to be kept safe from.

They are my family and...

Family first.

I will still marry. Just not to anyone in this family. It was only an interview—he never should have kept me. I'm going home. Besides, I know they expect me back by now. If I don't show my face in the next hour, they're going to come looking for me and start a war.

One my marriage is supposed to prevent.

It's a flimsy attempt, this proposed marriage arrangement. My vows would be a wall of smoke between the two families. Like I said earlier, one huff from a hot-headed captain, and *poof!* It's gone.

I glide across the room on the polished wood floors toward the door, planning my exit. My soft-soled shoes don't make a sound and I'm glad I snuck back to my room before I left and changed out of the ridiculous high heels my father forced me to wear. I should have been wearing a dress that was sleek and short and sexy, like what girls my age wear out to the clubs, clubs I've never been allowed to step foot in. But my brothers dressed me up like a middle-aged woman, trying to make me look older, knowing the head of the Bachman family is sleeping with the widow across the lake.

Laughing, my brothers called the widow a cougar and me a kitten.

They've forgotten how feisty kittens can be. We'll scratch your eyes out if we need to.

The pins at the back of my neck pull at the fine hairs there and I tug them out of the updo, letting my hair flow down over my shoulders silky and clean, now in waves from the silly chignon Mattia managed to create. I want to cut my hair short, but the men in my family won't let me.

Not until I've captured myself a husband.

I glance around the room, my heart taking a dissatisfied dip, knowing I have to leave it. It's gorgeous. The walls are white, and the one facing the lake and mountains is all windows, the glass spotless.

A four-poster frame—every little girl's dream—is covered in a fluffy white duvet and pillows piled up on the high bed. In the center of the wall across from the bed is a fireplace surrounded by smooth gray rectangular stones. It's gaslit, one you simply turn on with the press of a paddle switch instead of the messy wood fires we could burn at our house but never do. And the best part of all is that the walls on both sides of the fireplace are lined with...

Shelves and shelves of books.

Honestly? If the property didn't come with marriage to a man, I'd have jumped at the chance to be imprisoned here.

Set against the foothills of the Alps, the nearer craggy sides covered with thick evergreens and the mountains further in the distance rising into bright white snowcaps, the estate is nestled up to the edge of the lake. The water is a beautiful blue green, a deep aqua, a stunning contrast to the smooth white stucco and pale gray wooden shutters of the main home.

Four stories with a room built completely of glass coming off the back, showcasing nature's breathtaking backdrop of the lake and mountains.

They have this pool, a rectangle of soft-teal water, a stone patio surrounding it, a narrow line of shrubbery, and then there's the lake, so close you could toss a pebble from one body of water to the other.

And the gardens they brought me through, they remind me of my mother's before she died. Short green hedges cut into paths, the corners of the paths shaped into diamonds with open centers, rose bushes rising from within, the heady scent of their flowers lingering in the air, drifting through the open window of my room.

I inhale the scent, think of my mother, and calm my nerves as I tiptoe to the tall wooden door. I memorized the long halls of the estate when they brought me from his library to this room. To get here I went up twisting stairs, my hand sliding against an iron railing, my feet dancing against gleaming, polished wood treads. I know the way back.

Pressing my hands against the wood of the door, I listen for voices.

Nothing.

I don't know if it's my small size or my tendency to hold my tongue if I've not been spoken to, but once again, I've been underestimated. They haven't even put a guard at my door.

Seeing the bruises on my arm, maybe they assumed I wouldn't try to go home, that I wouldn't want to go back, but we all know what they say about assumptions.

You can stick 'em where the sun doesn't shine. An old Wild West phrase my American tutor taught me before the money ran out and we had to let him go too. I still have a hint of his accent though.

I turn the glass knob in my hand. A smile curls at my lips.

As I suspected...

Unlocked.

The Bachmans really don't know how to capture a princess in their towers, now do they?

LIAM

WHY AM I STANDING HERE?

At *her* door...

The little pet.

I'm late for my meeting with Widow Russo. She despises when I'm not there when I said I would be, and I hate rudeness as well. So, why am I here?

"Emilia?" I rap my knuckles against the wood three times and wait.

"Yes?" She sounds close, like she's right on the other side of the door.

"It's me. I'd like to speak to you a moment."

The door opens slowly. Did the knob not turn? Was she standing by the door when I arrived? Her golden head pops out between the door and the frame. She's taken her hair down and it falls in soft waves around her shoulders.

Her lashes flutter at me. "Yes?"

"May I come in?" I flatten my palm against the door.

She narrows her gaze at me. "Doesn't matter what I say, you're coming in either way, aren't you?"

"It is my house," is my answer to her question as I move past her. "And soon it will be your house too."

A curious look flashes over her face and she says nothing.

What am I doing here? I think of a quick excuse. "I'd like to introduce you to the single brothers I have living here with me at The Villa." Cannon's at the club but I shoot a text to the others, telling them to get their asses up here.

"They'll be here in just a minute." I stand in the center of the room, admiring the way the light flows in through the windows. She's got a spectacular view here of the lake and the mountains. I nod at the fully stocked shelves. "You like to read?"

She shrugs. "When I have time for it."

"You'll have plenty of that while we sort out the arrangement for your marriage to one of my brothers," I say.

We stand in a tense silence, her staring me down, me wondering what's taking them so damn long to get up here.

She plants a hand on her slim hip. "You mean while I'm trapped up here because you kidnapped me?"

"You haven't been kidnapped," I say, keeping my voice smooth. "I'm holding you. For your safety."

"What makes you think I'm safer here? I've heard what you Bachmans do to your women."

"Have you?" I take a step toward her and she shrinks back, her hand falling from her hip. "What have you heard?"

Her voice trembles, but she stands strong. "That you punish them if they disobey. How is that different than what goes on at my house?"

I can read in her face how very different her house is than mine.

"Your brothers are volatile, unstable, quick to anger. Can be useful for what we need in a mafia partner, but never for dealing with women. Bachman men have our own code. We are authoritative, command respect, and yes, we must be obeyed, but we are dependable. Stable." I give her a slow nod. "We can be trusted."

She cocks a brow. "And the punishment bit? You're leaving that out." Pink blooms rise in her cheeks. "I think I got a little taste on the road last night..."

I can't seem to stop myself, moving toward her almost like I'm watching myself from above, my actions in slow motion.

She stares up at me and I reach out, cupping the curve of her heated cheek against my cool palm. I have to bend down quite far, she's so tiny. I bring my lips to her ear.

She smells of vanilla and honey and wisps of her hair move as I speak low, lust-laden words against her skin.

"That part I can show you." I slide a hand along her lower back, cupping her ass and pulling her against me. "If you want."

Her body goes soft in my arms for the beat of a moment, then her weakness dissolves and she dons her cold, rigid, protective shell.

"I had enough of your show on the road, thank you very much." She shakes her head, hands flattening against my chest. "No, thank you."

"The offer stands." I pull away, the intoxicating scent that is her lingering in my senses.

She takes a backward step, crossing her arms over her chest as if to wrap herself away from me. Or retain the heat she felt against me.

"Don't hold your breath," she snaps.

"I won't." I make sure to hold her gaze. "And you, don't leave this room. Or I will show you. And next time, I won't ask."

She can't hide the little shiver that travels down her spine, ending in a telltale twitch of her thin shoulders.

There's a knock on the door. I step away from her. She takes a moment to smooth down her wrinkled dress.

"Come in," I call.

The single men pile in, a gathering of testosterone, designer clothing, and too much cologne. I introduce my blood brothers first, all but Cannon who's at the club working. "Tristan, Hunter, Dom, meet Emilia."

They saunter over to her, taking her hand in theirs.

Tristan shoves a long lock of hair back from his eyes, giving her that panther's grin he's known for. "Pleasure to meet you, ma'am. I'm not around much, I'm mostly on a boat, running... supplies... for the family, but if there's anything you need, please ask."

She gives a tight nod. "Thank you. I appreciate that."

She's got manners when she's not so pissed off.

Hunter approaches next. He's the one who told me in no uncertain terms that he will not marry. But now as he brings Emilia's hand to his lips in the soft kiss of a greeting, I wonder if he's having second thoughts about his bachelorhood. "Lovely to meet you."

Hunter's kind of a gentle cowboy type when out and about in town, but deadly and cunning in our world. Our mom must have had a sixth sense when she named him too, because he's our sniper, a god behind a scope. Ladies are disarmed by his charms and Emilia's no different. He lets her hand slip from his in a way that makes a blush rise in her face and my hands clench into fists.

"And Dom," I say, giving my shy, youngest brother a push forward. "Dom, meet Emilia." Dom has a cool head and thinks much deeper than other men his age. Right now, he's shadowing me, just learning the ropes. He's the closest to Emilia's age and with her fire and his calmness, they might be a good match.

He steps forward, giving her a nod and a sheepish grin. "You're... ah... really pretty."

"Thank you." She looks away.

Next come the three single men from the Brotherhood I brought to The Villa with us. They're from the Russo family in Southern Italy. Relatives by marriage to Widow Russo. A few years ago they joined the Brotherhood and further tied our alliance with their family.

Enzo's hair is lighter than the other Russo brothers, a sandy blond, but he has deep brown eyes. He's the eldest of the three Russo brothers who've joined. He's an artist—I have his paintings hanging through The Villa—but he doesn't talk much about it. Everything he wears looks good on him. Today he wears a close-cut gray jacket over a black T-shirt. He's a bit too dark and brooding for me to picture him with Emilia.

Leo and Po are the fourth and fifth of the brothers and with their broad shoulders and similar hair styles, I sometimes have a hard time telling them apart. They are gregarious, constantly egging one another on, going from laughing to fighting then back to laughing within the span of one conversation. Leo is slightly taller, his eyes green like Emilia's oldest brother's, with an edge to them but friendlier than Antonio's.

Po is the funnier of the two and always has a smile on his handsome face.

I'm closest to Po. He's brutal with his honesty but always manages to disarm me with his humor. He tells it like it is and I need someone like that in my corner.

She politely greets each one of them with a cool disinterest.

"Thank you, men." I stare at Emilia as they file out, Po giving me a curious gaze as he goes.

"Pretty girl," he whispers in my ear, a teasing tone in his voice.

"Perfect for you," I shoot back. I know what he implies. Po misses nothing and he's seen the way I look at her.

When they're gone, I make my way to the door.

I call over my shoulder to Emilia, "Tell Marta if there's something you need. Or want. Anything you want, you can have."

"My freedom?" she asks.

I turn back, catching her steely eyes, more gray than green now.

"Anything," I say, "but that."

I close the door.

3

E *milia*

THE MEN WERE ALL RIDICULOUSLY HANDSOME, POLITE, AND A FEW seemed to have a kindness in their eyes. One even made me blush with the way he touched my hand. But my eyes always traveled back to Liam's dark eyes.

Watching me.

He leaves, closing the door. I wait for a lock outside the door to click but it doesn't come. My fingertips go to my cheek, dragging over the skin that still tingles from his touch. He claims he's dependable, trustworthy.

But I know what he is. What they all are.

Men.

And they are not to be trusted. Men wield their power like they wield their hands, and they'll do anything to keep a woman in her place.

Which is anywhere below them.

No, thank you. I don't care for the unknown. I'll stick with my own kind. Brutal, but at least I know what to expect and how to handle them. These brothers of Liam's—who knows what they are really like?

I'll tell my father, my brothers, that we need to keep looking for a suitable match. Surely there is a softer, less domineering man in this mafia world for me to marry.

Now, to get home.

The door is unlocked. There are no guards. Does he really think he can deter me with a harsh tone and a gaze of steel?

I almost laugh, thinking of his threat.

Don't leave this room. Or I will show you. And next time, I won't ask.

Show me what? How he's different? How his punishments are morally superior to those of the men of my family?

Still, I can't deny the shiver he made run down my spine. I think back to the road and where his fingers wandered to, and the unwanted heat that flashed through my body at his touch, awakening my core with a deep, pulsing throb.

Men...

Can't live with them. And if you're a woman in our world?

Can't survive without them.

Without making a sound, I pull the door closed behind me, creeping down the hall. I slip down the curling stairs, exiting by a small door I find along the side of the hallway. Stepping out into the garden, I inhale the cool evening air laced with the heady scent of roses.

My house is miles from here, too far to walk. I could find a guard and beg for a ride, but I don't have anything to barter with. I could borrow a car, somehow... I've seen Liam's brothers out on the curving road that passes my house, speeding by in their Maseratis.

No one's ever taught me to drive. Wait. Horses. I know they have horses. My mother grew up riding and used to take me to her parents' house and teach me. After she died, for a while my father was able to afford private lessons. I can ride a horse bareback just fine.

I go in the direction where I saw outer buildings dotting their perfectly manicured landscape. As I near a long white building that resembles a stable, just much more pristine than any I've ever seen, I hear a whinny.

Inside the stable, I find a horse with a pale gray coat that looks slightly friendlier than the others. It lifts its head at the sound of my footsteps, looking directly at me. Like it's been waiting for me.

I reach my hand out and the horse nuzzles it as if eager to please. "Here we go, sweetheart. Can you help me with a favor?"

There's a skittering sound from the back corner of the quiet barn. It startles me, making me jump. My head jerks over my shoulder, expecting to find an angry man looming in the shadows.

It's just an orange tabby, its fur patchy from fighting. He looks at me, giving me a grumpy meow.

"I get it, buddy. I'm feeling the exact same way." He slinks over to me, rubbing at my ankles. I bend down, holding out my fingers. "You had a long day too?"

He lets me give him a couple scratches behind his ears, then gives me another, less grouchy meow and stalks off.

I loosen the metal hook from the clasp and open the stall door. "You ready to ride?" I smile at the horse, and it feels like he's smiling back.

Moments later, I'm riding. The strong horse beneath me, my fingers tangled in its mane, the sound of hoofbeats against the soft earth as we ride down the narrow forest path, hidden from the main road. It's exhilarating.

Maybe I'll keep riding.

Maybe I'll ride right past my house and never look back, leaving this wretched mafia life behind.

But when the end of my gravel drive comes into view, I know my idea is a fleeting fantasy. I try to be strong, but I'm weak, bowing to my loyalty. I turn the horse, trotting up to the house.

I reach the crumbling stone of the front steps and pull the horse to a stop. "Whoa."

Sliding down his smooth side, my feet finally touch the ground, my legs a bit wobbly from the ride.

"Thank you, friend." I pat his nose and smack him on the rear. "Go on home."

He gives me a look like he's asking me if I'm sure. I nod and he takes off, trotting toward the Bachman estate.

He'll make it home. Just like I did. Two animals bred in captivity.

I turn to the house.

It's starting to look dilapidated on the outside, dark green paint peeling from the wood siding, one of the black shutters hanging crooked. You can absolutely judge this book by its cover. When my mother died, my already dark father went to a black hole of a place, throwing around money like paper to buy men and expand his power. There was no money for anything else, and without my mom to stop him, her trust fund has been dwindling.

Soon, there will be no money left. Then all the men my father bought will leave. That's why he wants me married so quickly.

My mother would have made him let me wait for love.

The concept of love in this family died with her.

The house has been falling apart both on the outside, from lack of funding for the upkeep, and on the inside, from lack of her love.

My mother held this family together. She was our protector. She could soothe my father with her soft smile and one gentle touch to his forearm. She kept my father's temper under control, set the mood of the home, and created stability.

Now, I never know what waits for me on the other side of our front door. My fingers wrap around the cold metal knob.

I'm so lost, standing at the doorway of my father's house. I don't know what to do. I have no one to talk to.

My whispered words disappear in the wind. "Why did you have to leave, Mama? I need you."

Liam

THE SHEETS ARE COOL AGAINST MY SKIN AS I LIGHT MY CIGARETTE. The widow always has the most comfortable bed, sparing no expense on her linens. I never use her name, because it'd feel like a slight to her dead husband, a man I respected greatly who died in the line of fire several years ago.

My limbs feel loose, languid, the aftereffects of our intense moment together. I watch her, taking a drag from my cigarette, as she pulls the white sheet around her, sipping the last of her wine. As always, our talk turns to business as soon as we've taken care of our primal needs.

"How were your interviews?" She sets the crystal goblet on the nightstand, the lamplight hitting the etched glass.

She's a good listener and I have her full attention as I speak.

"They went well. There was some potential there, a few maybes for my brothers. Really, most of the girls were pretty but forgettable."

The Widow smirks. "Really? Not one girl was memorable?"

The pouty little smirk of the tiny blonde flashes through my mind. "There was this one... Emilia."

Widow Russo's spine straightens as she deepens the focus of her attention. "Your face."

"What about it?" I take another drag, careful not to drop flakes of ash on the sheets she imported from Egypt.

"It changed. When you said the girl's name."

"I don't think so. It was just the others were so meh. She stood out."

"How did she stand out?" Her voice is smooth as she digs.

Prickles of discomfort rise on my skin. "I don't know. She just did."

"Hmm..." The Widow gives me a smirk of her own.

I usually enjoy our talks. The Widow has a sixth sense, a talent for reading people's emotions, and is one of the few people in this world who can read me. Only now, her probing is making me uncomfortable, and the prickles creep further into my skin. Faced with the truth, I must admit to myself that when I was lying with the Widow this afternoon, more than once my mind went to Emilia.

Remembering my hands on Emilia's slight body as I whispered sweet threats into her ear on that road.

I shrug it off. "She was... noteworthy. I kept her afterward. She's at the house."

Her dark brows shoot up toward the cathedral ceilings. "You kidnapped her?"

"I'm detaining her. For safekeeping."

She lights her own cigarette. "And when her father wonders where she's gone to?"

"He can come to me and tell my why she has bruises on her arm."

"Bruises." She gives a dark laugh. "What's the problem? Bruises are a part of our life. Why do you care?"

"Violence outside the home, yes, it's part of our lives." My blood heats, thinking of Emilia's arm. "But violence inside the home is unacceptable."

"Says the man who loves nothing more than to cause pain to his women." She leans her head back, blowing a smoke ring into the air above her. "If you had a wife—"

"Which I don't and won't." My cigarette is almost gone, blue smoke rising into the air.

She presses on after taking a drag of her own smoke. "But if you had one and she disobeyed you, you'd inflict pain. Just like my late husband. Probably why I let you in my bed in the first place. Just to get a taste of what I had with him."

"The pain I dish out is followed by pleasure." I hold her gaze, giving her that wicked smile the women love. "I draw out a woman's deepest desire. To lose control to a man worthy of her submission. And I never leave a mark."

She crooks a brow at me.

"Well," I correct myself, "I rarely leave a mark."

"Just be careful with this one. You seem..." Her red lips wrap around the end of her cigarette, taking an inhale then blowing a smoke ring toward me as she looks me over. "Smitten."

I give a half-laugh. "That's a word I've never heard used to describe me."

She stubs out her cigarette in the bottom of her crystal wineglass, twisting it in dregs of purple wine. "That's why I'm saying to be careful."

She uses the tone of a discerning business partner, dishing out advice to keep a friend from making a bad investment.

If I was being careful, after meeting Emilia on the road that night, would I have ensured that she was on the top of my interview list just so I could see her one more time?

"Dom," I say, too quickly. I stretch over her body, adding my cigarette to hers. The embers fade the moment it hits the wine. "She'll be perfect for Dom."

.

Emilia

My father is storming the dimly lit foyer, pacing back and forth, his heavy boots rattling the single-pane windows as he stomps. Don't tremble, don't show weakness. Be fierce.

It's the safest way to deal with him.

"Tell me again. Exactly what he said and exactly what you did." His storm cloud-gray eyes turn on me and freeze me to stone.

"I told you. He asked me a few questions and then, he liked me so much, he tried to keep me, locking me away in a room. I snuck away. A family that would kidnap me is not one we want to align with. Surely, we can find someone else."

"Foolish girl," he roars. "They are quickly becoming the most powerful family in Italy and have wealth beyond anything we've dreamed of having. You should have stayed!"

"I—I thought you'd be angry with me if I didn't come home. That you'd look for me, that you'd retaliate..." My words trail off as I realize how stupid I've been.

My father doesn't care enough about me to start a war over my attempted kidnapping. He doesn't care for me at all. I'm just a paycheck to him now.

He throws his hands up in the air, his voice booming through the echoey room. "This is exactly what we wanted. Him to want you. If he kept you in a room, so be it. We'd have been that much closer to our goals. Look around you!"

Trying to appease him, I let my gaze travel around the room, taking in the burnt-out light bulbs in the chandelier over my head, the faded curtains, once a deep burgundy, now a hideous pink. The carpets that are threadbare and in desperate need of cleaning.

He leans in, the scent of whiskey surrounding me, spittle flying in my face as he pokes a sharp finger into me, just below my collarbone. "You are going back there. You are going to sneak back through the forest and get yourself back into that room before he finds out you're gone. Better yet, if he has found out you're gone, show yourself to him and beg, plead, offer yourself to him for forgiveness." The finger beats into my chest, deeper with each word. "I don't care what you have to do, just fix this."

The pain from his finger poking me seeps into my chest, his words building rage. Offer myself to him for forgiveness? Disgust fills me.

Fathers should protect their daughters, not whore them out to the highest bidder.

"Did I hear you correctly? You want me to offer to have sex with him?" The words blurt forth and I can't take them back.

"Don't be crass." He pulls his hand back and I know it's coming, but still, when the back of his hand hits my cheekbone, I'm shocked by the blinding pain that explodes across the side of my face.

I stumble backward, unable to control the watery tears that spring up in my eyes. I hate myself for showing weakness, for letting the tears roll down my face. My hand goes to my cheek.

He points to the door. "Now, get out. And don't come back until there's a ring on your finger." He turns, leaving me.

Antonio appears in his absence. He stands at the end of the dimly lit hall, the features of his face arranged in a calm, menacing mask. A chill creeps over my skin. "Don't you see your family needs you? How dare you come back here when he was ready to pay us for you."

His boots are heavy, but his glide is graceful and silent as he moves toward me.

I take a step back, closer to the door, words choking in my throat.

He's looming over me now, staring down at me with harsh eyes. I look away, knowing he hates the tears streaming down my face, that they'll only make him angrier.

His hand goes to my ribcage, slipping over the cheap material of the dress. The cold chill I felt before now turns to ice. I swallow back vomit as he moves his face a beat away from mine. "Now go back there and show him that you're worth every penny."

His hand moves to my waist, cupping it. He squeezes, hard, waiting for my answer.

Pain and shame and disgust shoot through me, roiling my stomach and making my head ache.

"Okay! I'll go." I hate myself for caving, for saying the words, for being too small to protect myself. No matter how many weights I lift, I'm no match for Antonio.

"Good." He parrots Dad's words. "And don't come back until there's a ring on that finger of yours. Little bird."

I stand there, my heart hammering, tears flowing freely down my cheeks, and wait for him to leave. When he's gone, I breathe easier.

My gym bag sits by the door, a clean change of clothes and my new sneakers hidden inside. All ready for the morning when I planned to beg Mattia, my brother closest in age to me and who finds me slightly tolerable, to take me with him to work out.

I grab the bag and fly through the door, letting it slam behind me.

I'm not going to the Bachman Estate.

And I'm not staying here.

There is no suitable match for me in our world. There are only these hard, domineering men of the mafia.

I've been tired of this life since the moment I was born into it, sheltered in this ever-darkening estate. The only good thing here was my mother. I was going to be loyal to my family. Marry for their benefit. But now, I just want to leave this house.

I don't know where I'm going but it won't be into the hands of another man who'll abuse me.

I take off running into the forest.

4

E *milia*

I CHANGE INTO MY LEGGINGS AND TEE AND THE PRETTY PINK AND GRAY sneakers, tossing the ugly dress and my ballet slippers into the gym bag. I stuff the bag under the roots of a fallen oak.

Now what?

I look around the dark forest, the sounds of croaking frogs and hooting owls echoing in my ears. My father's enemies' homes are on the other side of these woods. Guards pace their property day and night. In front of me, the lake, the road, and the Bachmans.

I have no friends, no money, and nowhere to go.

God, how stupid was I? Thinking I could just disappear. Tears creep up in my throat at my foolishness.

Now, I'm terrified.

I start out at an easy jog toward town, a place I'm not too familiar with, my cheek throbbing.

I've lived my whole life in our mansion. Our gardens were my playground, my brothers my only companions. When my mother was there, it was magical. I didn't want to be anywhere else.

She died when I was ten. My dad had no idea what to do with a little girl, other than protect her by keeping her on the property with hired staff to help.

The mansion became my prison. A housekeeper cooked our meals. American tutors were brought in to educate me while my brothers went to school. Even then, my father was planning my marriage. He wanted me to speak English, knowing that the Bachman family had united with the Russo family and was looking to expand to Northern Italy, that one day they would set up a branch of their business by the lake.

He lets me go to town sometimes, but only in the company of my brothers.

I pick my way over fallen limbs, my sneakers crunching against the dry leaves. I can go to the gym. They know me there. I'll tell them Mattia is right behind me with his membership card. I can hide out in the changing rooms until they lock up. Break protein bars out of the vending machine and sleep on a yoga mat while I figure out a plan.

I find the road, staying in the woods, and follow beside it toward town.

Peace comes over me, knowing I'll at least have a few hours to myself to clear my head. I slow my jog to a walk. Why hurry?

The sounds of the forest get spookier. I'm not a big fan of the woods. Not a single car has passed me. I step out onto the road. It feels safer. If a bear or a monster wants to come for me, at least I can see them first without the trees.

It's quieter now, and I begin to enjoy the walk, staring up at the moon through the leaves. It's pleasant, this burst of freedom. Being alone, for once. Making a decision of my own—

"Shit!" My toe catches a broken piece of pavement and I fall to the ground, smacking my palms against the hard surface as my knees hit it.

I take inventory of my injuries. Nothing. Just a little dirt on my palms. See, Emilia? You're fine. You can take care of yourself—

The sound of a car fills the air. It's coming fast. Bright headlights burst around the corner, shining right in my face.

"Double shit!" I stand, pushing myself up off the pavement. The car is so close now. I don't recognize it as one of ours. I'm afraid I may not get off the road in time. It might hit me.

I run off the road, my feet hitting the soft ground. Who is this? One of my father's enemies? Are they trying to hit me? What will they do if they catch me? A massive black SUV comes to a squealing stop beside me.

I don't look back, willing my body to break out into a flat-out sprint over the crunching leaves.

I don't even make it six feet before strong arms wrap around my torso, pulling me back.

No. Oh no. My heart pounds in my ears, perspiration dotting the back of my neck. I'm frozen in fear, but I fight to break my way out of the ice.

"Let me go!" I stomp my foot on top of my assailant's, but my heel lands on the hard steel toe of his boot, inflicting no pain.

A familiar, rumbling voice fills my senses, bringing every inch of my flesh to life. It's him.

"I thought I told you to keep your runs to the gym."

"I'm on my way now. If you'd let me go!"

Hard hands grab my shoulders, forcing me to turn and face my fate.

"I also told you not to be out here alone again." He looms over me, a storm cloud of rage. "How naïve are you? Running off into the woods, no coat, no supplies, no phone. Your father's enemies prowling the borders of your lands? What were you thinking?"

Was I?

Thinking?

No. My father's words ring in my mind. Foolish girl. Am I glad it's Liam and not my father's enemies? I'm not sure which one brings me more danger. I think of his promise to show me how he punishes his women if I ran away. My tongue feels thick and dull in my mouth. I bow my head, letting my hair hide my face.

I don't know what to say.

He gives my shoulders a hard shake. "Talk to me. What the hell are you doing out here? I told you I never wanted to see you on this road again."

I remember why I left my father's house and ran into the woods. "I don't want to be sold to you and your brothers and I don't want to be beaten down by my father and brothers anymore." I shake my head, trying not to tear up. "I don't want any of you."

"You may not want us, but you need our protection. You think you're in pain now? Living in the safety of your father's house? You have no idea what kind of danger you'd be in if a captain from another family laid their hands on you—"

"Safety?" I turn my face, showing him the fresh welt I know has risen on my cheek. My father has a talent of striking without leaving a bruise, but surely there's a mark. "What makes you think I'm safe there?"

"Who did this?" His fingertips drag over the skin along my jawline, careful to avoid the tender flesh. Fury fills his gaze as it travels over my face. "Who did this?"

"Who do you think? My dad. When he heard his little cash cow ran off, he hit me. Told me to go back to you and do whatever I needed to get you to take me back. He's only after your money, you know that, right?"

"Of course he is. That was the deal. My money for your father's alliance. I need his men." He nods at my cheek. "They're vicious."

"Yeah." I laugh at the irony. "They were trained by my dad."

"Still, you were safer home than you are in these woods." His hand slips to my chin, capturing it between his forefinger and thumb. "Regardless, I told you not to leave that room, little pet."

Little pet...

The way he says *little pet* makes me want to kill him. But he's right. I'm nothing but a little pet. Raised, sheltered, having limited contact with the outside world, our crumbling mansion my cage. An animal to be sold by my father.

Warring emotions swirl in my belly when I think of Liam's big, clean, sun-filled home. The room with the fireplace and the books. His promise to be dependable and stable. I can handle the pain of his punishments.

I have nowhere else to go. This mafia king might be harsh, controlling, demand obedience, and be quick to punish, but he's not like my father or Antonio who are ruled by their tempers. Liam told me that I can trust him, and I believe him.

Does it even matter if I can't trust him?

I have no one else.

"We found you gone, and I went looking for you. Now, put your hand in mine and I will take you home and show you what it means to disobey a Bachman man." He holds out his hand, big and strong but controlled.

What do I do?

Run further into the woods? Go back to my father's only to be back-handed, a matching bruise on the other cheek, and sent away a second time?

Or...

Do I put my hand in his?

He's patient. Holding his hand out. Steady. Open. Waiting.

"Emilia. Now, please. Don't make me wait. That would be rude, and I don't have patience for it. I despise rudeness."

The command in his tone makes my hand lift in the air. He wants my consent, my submission. I place my hand in his. He wraps his fingers around mine, sealing my fate.

He lifts my hand to his mouth, brushing his lips over it. "There's a good girl. Come with me. I'll show you where I take you when you've been bad."

My fingers tremble, the uncertainty of what's to come making my belly flip and flop, my insides twisting and turning. I think of those secret books under my bed. My anxiety laces with excitement. I can't help it. I should only be filled with fear but the truth is, curiosity and desire fill me.

Have I spent too many lonely nights alone reading? Is that why my panties are dampening, my heartbeat quickening? Or is my body demanding from me what I've only teased my mind with: a big, strong man to take control of me, demanding my submission.

The black SUV waits for us, the driver standing guard by the door.

"Up you go, little one."

I pause, one sneaker on the running board of the massive car, staring at him. "Little but not weak."

Dark eyes hold mine. He nods. "Little but not weak."

I let him help me into the car.

The backs of my legs smooth along the cool, velvety black leather. He closes the door.

For a beat I'm alone. I sink back into the cushion, letting out the breath that I feel like I've been holding since I snuck out of his house.

The men enter the car, driver behind the wheel, Liam in the passenger seat.

My palms go damp, my heart fluttering against my breastbone.

I have the whole ride to sit in hot, prickling anticipation, wondering what bad girls get.

LIAM

I'LL HAVE MARTA ATTEND TO HER FACE. I WANT TO KILL HER FATHER for hitting her. Wouldn't really be the best way to start out our alliance, would it? Besides, his business with her is over.

She's my problem now.

And what a big fucking problem she is for such a tiny thing.

I've got four men eyeing her from the balcony, each wanting a piece of the eye candy as she steps down from the SUV. She's piqued their interest. In the morning, my brothers will want to know who she's going to.

Just like the other night when I caught her running, I find her breathtaking.

The light glitters off the natural gold strands in her hair. Her color-shifting eyes have gone green in the night sky. Moonbeams highlight her high cheekbones, the beginnings of a bruise appearing on one. The curve of her face like a crescent moon, dipping into her dimpled chin, full, pouty, rose-colored lips always twisted in a sneer of distrust.

Her body is firm and compact but under the tight spandex of her black leggings the form of her figure shows itself, her shapely legs rising into a heart-shaped ass, the fullest curve resting at the tops of her slim thighs.

Small round breasts sit high on her chest, the slightest outline of perky nipples showing through her thin, cropped tee. A slice of pale midriff shows as she stretches her leg down to step to the ground. I'm happy to see the shoes I sent on her feet.

She catches me staring, her lips curling in a *caught you* smile, knowing for a moment, she holds the upper hand in our game of power.

Fuck.

I run my hand over the back of my neck, turning away from her. I stare up at my brothers instead. "Cut your moon bathing short, princesses, and get back to work." Is that jealousy in my tone, wanting their wandering eyes off her body?

They laugh, elbowing one another and exchanging jibes as they leave the balcony.

If it's jealousy, it's misplaced, because it's for a girl that I'm going to marry off to one of them.

What the hell is wrong with me? I'll punish her so she knows the rule of this house and what happens when she breaks it. Afterward, I'll go to the Widow for the heady release she offers me.

Then, with my head clear, I'll choose the right brother and contact her father with the final terms of the marriage agreement. When he comes to sign, I'll make it known to him that if he ever lays a finger on his daughter again, I'll end him.

For now, my focus is to set this little girl straight and make sure she knows the rule. It's simple. There's only one.

Do as I say.

But she's having a hard time with it, so I'll teach her to be good.

"Come." I head to a smaller guesthouse that sits beside the main one.

She glances in the direction I walk with unsure eyes. "Where are we going? My room was in the other building."

"To a special place where I have everything I need," I say, "to punish a naughty girl."

"Oh." Her voice trembles, all her sassy remarks drying up.

Andre opens the door for us, clean light from the kitchen making a line over the dark earth. I step back for her to enter first.

Marta waits in the foyer, hovering by the credenza, wringing her hands then wiping them on the pink apron that's tied to her slim waist. I texted her from the car, filling her in on Emilia's situation.

"How bad is it, dear?" Marta peers over the rims of her silver glasses then flinches when she sees Emilia's cheek. "Come with me. I'll get you fixed right up. And I've got dinner waiting on the table for you too."

Emilia gives me a questioning glance, wondering if I mean to make her miss her dinner too.

"Go." I nod toward the kitchen. "We can have our chat after you eat and Marta helps you."

She gives me a tiny nod, following Marta.

Let her eat.

I have all night.

I head to the room to prepare.

She will learn to obey.

———————

EMILIA

THE MEAL MARTA'S PREPARED SMELLS OF WARMTH AND COMFORT, two things I'm in desperate need of. I sink into my chair, icicles running down my spine, but I can only pick at the untouched food with the prongs of my fork.

"Please," she says, eyeing me as she prepares her first aid supplies. "Eat. Even if it's only a few bites."

"It was really nice of you to make this for me." I dip the fork into the creamy potatoes and pop them into my mouth. Buttery and delicious. "Thank you. It's very good."

I think of the food we eat at home. The chef was the last servant my father let go. I've been making sandwiches for our dinners ever since.

Marta slides into the seat beside me. "May I?" She holds up a cloth filled with ice.

I feel bad, her having to attend to me like this. "I can do it."

"I want you to eat." She holds the towel to my cheek gently, but I still flinch when it makes contact.

"Thank you."

It's so tender, her touch, her voice, the way she holds the cloth to my skin as I eat the homemade food she's prepared for me. A soft, maternal energy emanates from her, something I haven't experienced in a long time. I push down the tears that threaten to come.

For Marta's sake, I take a few more bites of potatoes, chewing slowly. The food sits heavy in my stomach, cold dread settling around it.

I lay down my fork.

"Marta," I say. "Um... what do the Bachman men, like, *do,* you know... for like..."

She pats my hand. "Don't worry, sweetie. You'll survive. You really did get yourself into some trouble, though, didn't you? I haven't seen Mr. Bachman's face quite that red in a long time. Oh my, the language when he found your room empty—" She stops herself, realizing she's only making me more nervous. "You'll be fine. These men can't seem to keep the women away, so it can't be all that bad, can it? The women in this town are dying to be in your shoes, marrying a Bachman."

"How many women does he have?" The question pops out of my mouth before I realize I'm thinking it.

"Oh!" Marta's eyes widen behind her round glasses. "Um. Well, ah. The brothers, they have beautiful young ladies in and out of here all the time. I can barely keep up with them, but Liam—you are asking about Liam, correct?"

Embarrassment flows through me as I answer. "Yes. I mean, I guess."

She shakes her head. "He has a lady friend across the lake that he visits occasionally, a widow, but Liam, he doesn't date. It's a shame, because he'd make a fine husband, but I don't think he trusts himself to love after what happened—" Her face goes pink. "Oh gosh, what am I saying?"

What *is* she saying? "After what?"

Her eyes snap to the doorway. "Mr. Bachman! We were just finishing up. Let me get our guest some dessert and then—"

How long has he been standing there?

His eyes are heavy on my face. "Only good girls get dessert, Marta. You know that."

Shame dances down my spine and I have to look away.

Marta gives a nervous laugh. "Well, you can't hold it against me for trying. It's my famous apple pie and I'm sure Emilia would love a piece."

He leans against the frame of the door, crossing his arms over his chest. "No. Dessert."

"I'll save some. How about that?" She hops up, gathering my dishes as she moves around the table, patting my shoulder as she passes me.

He holds up a finger, crooking it and beckons me. "Come here, Emilia. Come with me."

I have no choice but to rise from my chair, knees made of jelly, heart thumping in my ears. Potatoes churning in my belly.

"Come here and take your punishment, little pet."

My fear is distracted by a scratching sound. My eyes travel toward the full glass kitchen door that leads to the garden. "I'm not the pet."

5

L *iam*

"WHAT ARE YOU LOOKING AT?" I FOLLOW HER GAZE. GOD, NOT THAT damn cat. The scroungy orange tabby that hangs around the barn sits at the back door, staring at Emilia through the glass.

She looks up at me, a little pout on her lips.

Is she serious?

She stares at me, then at the cat, then back at me.

"No. No way. That thing is filthy. Probably covered in fleas. Let's go. Now."

I don't miss the last look she gives the cat, like she's making a secret promise between them.

"Mark my words. That cat will not be coming in any of my houses. Not now. Not ever."

"We'll see." She brushes past me. "You said this will be my house too."

I grasp her shoulders, pulling her back into me. "It will be. And you'll follow the house rules."

I take her hand in mine and lead her from the kitchen. We walk down the long hall and as we pass the front door, she does exactly what I expect her to.

Runs.

She tears her hand from mine and breaks toward the door. I don't mind. I like the chase. For the second time this evening, I run after her, lock my arms around her torso, and pull her back into me. "You want to run, little girl? I'll only catch you. Try that again and I'll order my brothers to come watch me punish you. Would you like an audience?"

She goes frozen in my arms, terrified I'll carry out my threat. And I will if she tries this again. But she won't.

She trembles against me, shaking her head. "No. Please. Not that."

"Then for once since I've met you, try to be good."

I let her go, turning my back to her to show her I know she won't run again. She follows behind me down the hallway. We take the back staircase, the one that leads to the half-story above the guesthouse.

The ceiling is high, but the room narrow as the roof peaks, coming down in a triangle. It's my favorite room on the property. The walls are white; a bay of square dormer windows overlooks the mountains, moonlight shining through them, casting a glow over the soft white carpeting.

"Take off your shoes," I say, slipping off my own and setting them down, toes against the baseboard.

She gives me a curious look, tugging at the heels of her sneakers. She lines up the little pink sneakers neatly side by side.

Her eyes travel up to the white globe lights hanging from the ceiling, giving off a soft glow. Leafy green plants fill the corners of the room, set on wooden tables. There's a low blue velvet sofa.

"This," she says, "is the room?"

I cross over to the wall, placing my hand on the black metal piece of abstract art that hangs there, its lines crisscrossing, intertwined with one another. I grab the handle, giving it a good tug.

"This"—the door slowly creaks open, a sliver of pale light creeping across the carpet—"is the room. We have a kink club too, but I thought you'd prefer something a little more private for your first session."

"My first?" she asks. "Will there be more?"

"Judging by the fire in you," I laugh, "many more."

"And a club? What kind? You guys have your own kinky club tucked away somewhere—"

"Inside, please." I open the door fully.

She moves past me, stepping over the threshold.

God, seeing her here in this space... Adrenaline rushes through me, my blood heating.

I lift the hem of my shirt, pulling it up and over the back of my head. I toss it to the floor.

Her gaze goes wide, cheeks flushed as she takes in my chest. "Come here."

She's practically shaking as she crosses the room to meet me. I can almost smell the mix of terror and desire that burns off her skin like a fever. Good. The more fear she has of me, the more often she'll obey and the safer she'll be.

It makes me hard.

She looks up at me with those gray-green eyes. Even though she's trembling, she manages to hold my gaze and turn her lips into that smirk of hers. It'd anger me but I know how quickly it will be replaced with her cries, begging me to stop.

"Take off all of your clothes."

She jumps back. "What? No! What if you…"

"I won't. Take off all your clothes. Now."

"Can I take a shower first?"

"No."

"Well, can you tell me what to expect at least?" Her trembling fingers go the hem of her shirt, an attempt to look like she's obeying. She's stalling.

"You can expect to be punished."

Her voice squeaks. "Do I get a safe word or something?"

A dark chuckle rises from my throat. "Where did you hear that term?"

She rolls her eyes. "I have the internet, you know. eBooks. Ever hear of them? I know that a girl gets a safe word."

"Safe word?" I shake my head. "I don't do safe words. You are not in charge. I am. I'll decide when you've had enough and judging by how you're choosing to speak to me and roll your eyes at me, it's going to be awhile before you've had enough."

She looks up at me with wide eyes.

"Now strip."

EMILIA

MY HANDS ARE SHAKING. I CAN'T DO THIS. I WON'T DO THIS.

I won't take off all my clothes and let him do whatever the hell he wants to my naked body. I'm a virgin... I can't lose my virginity like this, can I?

He said he wouldn't. I cling to his word, hoping he is as he said, a man I can trust.

I glance around the room. The mysteries of sex surround me. Sure, I've stumbled upon dirty books on the internet, I've used my imagination to try and dream of myself in the scenarios I've read, but fumbling under the sheets with my inexperienced fingers, my eyes closed, imagining a man? It's nothing like this.

It'd be sexy in an "I've been locked away since before puberty and never even been kissed" kind of way if it wasn't so damn scary.

The walls are midnight blue. The color would be pretty if tools for punishment didn't hang from them. Displays, surrounded by empty gold picture frames, are organized around the room like the tools are works of art. One long, rectangular gilded frame surrounds paddles of different sizes and shapes. An oval picture frame holds blindfolds. It's almost beautiful. There are items I've never seen before. Set into the wall are shallow shelves and on them sit metal... things... shaped like teardrops.

Low couches line the walls, their fabric a crushed gold velvet. A massive chandelier with bulbs that look like candles hangs over our heads, filling the room with a soft glow. In the center of the hardwood floor is a thick metal square.

What it does, I'm not going to stay to find out. I've got to get out of here.

What do I do? Scream? Run for the door? Hope the tomcat comes to my rescue?

He's blocking the only exit and besides, I have no idea how to work it. Judging by the weird way he opened it in the first place, I'm guessing it was made to lock naughty girls in from the inside.

I have to attack. I stare at him. The bare muscled chest, the big biceps he's already captured me with twice tonight, stare back at me.

I try to remember what I learned from the self-defense class I snuck in at the gym. Knee to the crotch. Gouge out the eyes.

He senses my planning. He flashes me a grin that could be the Devil's. "While you're busy not getting undressed, plotting your escape, I'd like to draw your attention to the couches."

My gaze goes back to the sofas. Whatever that black metal square in the floor does, it's centered under the chandelier, the couches set around facing it. It's comfortable seating.

It's meant for an audience, isn't it?

He flips a switch on the wall. A modern take on classical music fills the room, a slow, melodic piano swelling into a livelier wave of notes, joined by violins as they beat out the fast pace.

His dark eyes flash a warning. "My brothers love this music."

His brothers... who he'd love to invite to watch.

My stomach flips over below my ribs. My knees are already jelly. "I..." My throat tightens, choking off my words.

I'm trapped.

My clothes have to come off. I must take them off. While he watches.

My only other choice is to fight a battle I know I won't win, then have his brothers come and watch the whole shameful thing, whatever it is he's planning on doing to me, and then there'll be a roomful of strange men observing my naked body.

I choose the monster that I know.

I lift my shirt, taking it off and tossing it onto his. The window is open, and a breeze blows in, cool night air making my skin rise with chill bumps. The ends of my hair flutter around my shoulders.

I fumble with my bra, unhooking it in the back. I let it slide to the floor, not covering my breasts with my hands.

Why bother?

My eyes slide to his face, and I catch a hunger in his eyes, an unsureness in the determined set of his jaw, like he's clenching his teeth to stop himself...

From what?

Admiring me?

No.

The cold air comes, awakening my nipples. They rise in the night air, standing on end at the peak of my small, firm breasts. I'm standing bathed in the warm candle glow, my hands at my sides, and I stare at him, staring at me.

He's not just admiring. He's lusting.

He wants me. Badly.

The thought makes hope brim in the center of my chest. Maybe... just maybe... this little pet might hold some power in a man's world after all.

The moment breaks. His voice comes over the music, gruff and filled with what I can't be sure of but what I assume is desire. "Lose the rest."

Let me test my theory. Let me play with this newfound power. I intentionally hold his gaze as I bring my fingers to the waist of my leggings. I push them down over my hips, careful to leave on my panties. The leggings fall to my ankles. One at a time, I tug my feet from them, having to break his gaze just long enough to rid myself of the pants. I toss them to the side and stand there.

Naked, save for the pair of simple white cotton panties I wear. I leave my arms hanging loose, cock my head to the side, look up at him from under my dark lashes, and I smile.

I drag the tip of my tongue over my bottom lip.

He gives a groan, a hand rising to rub at the back of his neck.

A heady thrill splashes over me. I've won. I've taken some tiny sliver of power back—and lose it all with his next words.

"Leave the panties," he says. "I'll take them off myself. Come here."

And he's grabbing me in those strong arms of his, bringing me to him. He stares down at me, heat and electricity snapping in the air between us. He leans down closer.

My God. He's going to kiss me.

My first kiss will be from a monster.

LIAM

THAT LOOK IN HER EYES WHILE SHE STANDS THERE STARING AT ME, licking her lips, her nipples hard, beg to be fondled and kissed just as much as her pouty mouth. I need to have my tongue in her mouth, to see if she tastes as warm and fiery as I think she does.

What the hell am I doing? I snap my head back just before I let my lips press against hers. Kissing is *not* part of my plan.

I grab her hand, pulling her to the center of the room. A push of a button on the remote that's hidden in my pocket, and the metal square shifts to the side.

I watch her eyes widen as the black leather pommel horse rises from the floor.

"What," she whispers, her sexy façade gone, replaced by her trembling, "is that?"

Her innocence, her fear, come off her like steam off the road during a summer storm, and I bathe in them. This Emilia, the soft, unsure one, this one I know how to handle.

The siren, I can do without. It makes me feel too... It just makes me feel something for her that I don't have room for in my life.

I'm going to punish her, to rob her of that sexy Emilia facade, the one who knows I want her, until that girl is gone and all that's left is my broken little pet.

I grab her shoulder, pushing her toward the horse. Her stomach presses against the leather. I've guessed perfectly for her height. I press a hand between her shoulder blades, folding her over the curve of the top of the saddle. Her hair hangs down around her face, her fingers grabbing the leather.

I circle a hand around her right wrist, pulling her arm out. I run my hand along the back of the horse, finding the metal cuff there. I snap it around her wrist, good and tight.

"Hey!" Panic rises in her voice. "What are you doing?"

"Helping you. I know you like to run. I also know you don't want my brothers in here." I move to her other wrist, snapping that one in its cuff. "Say, 'thank you, sir.'"

"Are you serious? You really want me to call you—"

I cut off her words with a sharp slap of her ass over her little white panties.

"Holy shit! That hurt."

She has no idea what is coming. "That was just a little swat. A friendly reminder to hold your tongue."

She sucks in air between her teeth, breathing through the sting.

"Now, thank me for cuffing you to the horse. For tying you down so you can't run, and I don't have to bring my brothers up here to watch."

"Thank you." Hatred is laced at the edges of her words. "Sir."

I smooth a hand over her back, her arms that hang down, pinned to the horse. I leave a trail of chill bumps in the wake of my touch. "Do I need to lock your ankles in as well?"

"That's a... thing?"

"Yes. I have everything. Ankle locks, nipple clamps, anal beads."

I can picture how much she's blushing right now; how hot her cheeks are with embarrassment. She's never experienced any of this. And I shouldn't be the one punishing her, touching the body of my soon-to-be sister-in-law so intimately.

It's not appropriate for me to strip her naked and punish her ass. I know this.

For once, I don't care what's appropriate.

It's going to be me.

I'll be the first one to show her.

I will be the one to introduce her tight young body to our world of pleasure and pain.

For one night, she's mine.

6

E *milia*

I'VE NEVER HAD A MAN SEE ME NAKED BEFORE. HIS EYES ON MY breasts I could handle, especially when I saw the way he was looking at me. I realized there's power in the beauty of them. But now, his fingers are tugging at the waistband of my panties, and I can't breathe.

Can't breathe.

The leather is cool against my skin, my breasts flattened against the velvety cushion, my nipples achingly hard, rubbing against the smoothness as I move, checking the cuffs for weakness.

They're locked tight.

I'm totally powerless against him and the realization weighs down on me, heavy and sickening. Fingers rake along my skin and the fabric that covers me. Inch by inch, he drags the cotton panties over my ass, settling them just under my curves. He leaves them tucked at the tops of my legs.

Humiliating.

More cool breeze caressing my naked ass.

I think of the books under my bed, the men in their pages. Liam is every bit one of those men, and I tremble in anticipation like the heroines of the stories. I watch as he walks across the room, going to the oval picture frame. He pulls down a black silk eye mask, one I'd picture movie stars wearing to sleep. I duck my head back down as he comes to me.

"Let's take away your sense of sight so you have one less thing distracting you from your punishment, shall we?"

He slips the mask over my eyes. The room goes dark, the crescendo of violins rising and falling around me.

His palm flattens against my lower back, his hand smoothing down past my waist until it rubs over my ass, the caress ending in a cupping of the fullness of my left ass cheek. I hold back a moan, everything in me telling me this feels good.

It's thrilling, terrifying, to be powerless. The swell of the music, the darkness behind the mask, the coolness of the breeze, the slickness of the leather, the feeling of metal cuffs biting into my wrists.

His hand holding my curves.

My senses go into overdrive.

He releases me, pacing the floor behind me, his gaze heavy on my naked body. "My, my, my. Where to begin?" His hand comes back to my ass, stroking it softly. He raises his palm in the air and I tense, sensing it hovering over me. I wince, waiting for the slap.

When it comes, to my surprise, instead of a scream, I let out a soft moan, relaxing into the horse.

The spank... feels... *good.*

Warm and tingly... making me... wet.

The light sting spreads over my skin, traveling right between my thighs, making me grateful he's left the panties there to absorb the wetness that flows from me. He spanks me again, another soft slap that awakens my skin.

I like it. Why do I like it?

Shame fills me as he starts to spank me lightly, repeatedly, alternating cheeks, focusing his sexy smacks on the center and bottom of my ass. I moan again, shifting my weight on the balls of my bare feet as an aching comes, heavy in my core. My sex pulses, wanting to be touched. In the peak of my shame, I press myself harder against the saddle of the pommel horse, looking for some relief.

This is worse than if it were painful. He's doing this on purpose. Filling me with need. Making me weak with desire. Forcing my body to want him.

I'm surprised by the voice that appears, hot and lust-filled, right by my ear.

"Are you going to hump my pommel horse, you naughty little thing?"

"N—no," I protest with a shaky voice. "I was just moving my feet."

He drags his hand over my ass, giving the fullest part at the bottom little pats, cupping my flesh in his palm. "Liar."

"My legs were falling asleep," I say.

"I think you like your spanking too much. I think it's making my pet's little kitty all wet and hot and needy and you're looking for some release." His fingers fight their way into the gap of my pushed-together thighs. "Let me see if I'm right. Spread your pretty legs for me."

He's going to... touch me... check me for the wetness we both know is there... And I must obey him?

I give a groan, moving my feet apart to give him better access to my sex.

He tugs my panties down further, letting them fall to the floor. I kick them from my ankles, putting my spread-apart feet back in place.

"You're learning, aren't you?" The roughness of the denim of his jeans brushes against the backs of my bare thighs as he comes behind me. His fingers dip between my thighs, stroking at my wetness. I suck in my breath, his touch an explosion of pleasure as he drags his slick finger up, touching my clit. "See, good things can happen when you obey."

A shudder tears through me, a whine creeping up in the back of my throat.

"Yes, sir," I breath out, wanting to beg for more of his touch.

My good behavior is rewarded with the tip of his finger teasing my entrance. Oh my God... having him touch me is nothing like when I tried myself. His touch is strong and sure but light, teasing my entrance. I move my hips like I can force him inside me, but it doesn't work that way, does it?

He has all the power.

"Do you want me inside you, pretty girl? Do you want to feel my fingers inside you, filling you up, stroking you while I rub your clit with the pad of my thumb? Fucking you with my fingers till you come all over my hand. Is that what you want?"

My knees were already weak but his growly voice has me leaning harder against the pommel horse so I don't collapse.

"Yes, God, please."

And his fingers disappear, his hand whipping away from my body. "Naughty girls don't get to come."

My sex aches, heavy and pulsing like my heartbeat has moved from my chest to between my thighs. *"Nooo..."*

"Yes. Instead of my fingers in your pussy like good girls get, you want to know what you're getting? What bad girls like you get, the ones who disobey and do silly things like run alone into the woods. Do you know what they get?"

"No." I shake my head, my hair swishing around my face. "I don't."

"My plug pushing past your tight little asshole, filling up your ass." He slaps my ass. Hard. The pain is blinding, and it makes me gasp. "That's what you get."

He's going to put something in my ass! I should have known based on his intrusive finger that night on the road. Still...

"Plug? God, what's that? What's a plug?"

The eye mask is pulled back from my face, nestling at the top of my head. I blink as the light fills my gaze. He's holding something in front of me. One of those teardrop-shaped metal things that was sitting on the shelf.

My gaze snaps up to his. "That. Is not going inside me."

"It is." The... thing disappears from my view, then I feel it, cold and hard, pressing against the cleft of my ass. "It's going in your bottom and then you're going to sit down in the kitchen, and eat your pie, your pretty little ass filled with my plug."

"You want me to wear that... thing. And sit and talk to Marta!"

There's the sound of a cap popping open. The plug leaves my ass. There's a squelching sound. Then his fingers are walking between the tops of my inner thighs, creeping up to my asshole, parting my cheeks.

"Spread those gorgeous legs for me."

Hiding a whine, I move my feet further apart. I can't believe this is happening, that he's going to put something inside me, back there. I'd take the paddle over this any day. But he knows that, doesn't he?

He wants to punish me in a way that will bring the most shame, not pain. He wants my humiliation, the hot wave of embarrassment rushing through my body, as my penalty for running away.

Cold jelly touches my skin, his finger pressing against the tight ring of muscles at the entrance of my ass. I've never even had a man's fingers inside me and now he's putting something foreign, cold, and hard inside my ass. *Unbelievable.* My teeth sink into my bottom lip to hold back the cry I want to give.

"Let's get this tight little hole lubed up so I can get this inside you." A shaky breath catches in my chest as he pushes his finger past my unwilling muscles.

"Oooh... unn..." He pushes his finger in up to the first knuckle, then pulls it back out. Adding a second finger to the first, he pushes them both inside of me.

My skin burns as it stretches, obeying his thick fingers. It feels so strange, this pressure, having him inside me like this. Desire drives down in my core, a thick feeling of wanting his fingers inside my sex, touching me.

But even deeper, as he pumps his fingers in a place I never even thought someone would go, there's another layer, an emotional one, wanting him to take me in his arms, for *him* to be inside me.

I lay over the pommel horse, tears pricking at the backs of my eyes. I'm lonely and alone. One more man wanting to control me. Only this is the closest anyone has gotten to me.

I want more from him.

And that scares me.

I should be screaming, fighting, kicking, trying to run away. And here I am, spreading my legs further, letting him push this thing inside me, all the while wanting to lose my virginity to him, to have him hold me in his arms to—

"Oh my God. Oh my God."

His fingers leave me, and I feel despairingly empty. Then, the cold, slippery head of the plug replaces his fingers, pushing inside of me. It's burning, my ass stretching to full capacity as he moves the toy inside it. My body pushes it back, then lets it in, over and over, till it's almost all the way inside me.

"This," he says, giving the plug a twist, "is the smallest one I have. Run away again and see that gold one on the shelf?"

My ass is so full, I couldn't possibly take anything bigger. I turn my head to the right, toward the shelf. My eyes widen as I see the plug he speaks of. "The gold one? It's massive."

He gives my ass a spank so hard tears pop up in my eyes. White heat flashes over my face as the pain settles in where he's smacked my ass. Is he going to keep spanking me this hard? I don't know that I can take it. Fear ricochets through me.

"It is massive," he says. "And if you don't want to feel it in your ass, be a good girl."

He leaves me. His footsteps echo through the room. What's he doing? Where's he going?

I shift my feet, trying to get used to the weight of the plug. He comes back, relief washing over me as he touches me with a soft cloth, wiping at my skin to clean up the excess jelly.

His fingers circle my wrists, unlocking the cuffs. He helps me up from the horse.

"Ooh..." Upon standing, the plug's existence takes on a whole new feeling. Heavy and uncomfortable. I can't help it, my ass muscles clench around the plug, feeling its heft. As my ass tightens, deep longing tears through me from the contrast of my sex being empty .

I don't want to face him. I can't. The aching wanting in my still-untouched sex melds with the wanting, dull aching in my chest.

I feel desire and hatred and stimulation from the plug and lack thereof from his too-few touches and I want to kill him and I want him to hold me and I don't know what I want. Tears prick at my eyes.

Nooo...

I'm so humiliated already, crying would only push me over the edge. I'm so freaking embarrassed and naïve and I don't even know exactly what it is my body is begging for—

"Hey." His hand smooths up my cheek. "Are you crying?"

"No," I sniff, my fingers going to my eye, brushing away the tear that threatens to fall. "I'm not crying."

"Look at me."

When I look up at him, it's through watery eyes, the tears making his face all blurry. He holds my cheek, the pad of his thumb brushing over my chin.

"Hey."

Have my tears caused him a moment of weakness? For once, he doesn't seem to know what to say and neither do I.

He stares at me for a beat, his dark gaze focused on mine as if he's weighing a heavy decision, looking for answers in my eyes. Anger flashes through his dark irises like I've pissed him off all over again.

Finally, he shrugs. "What the hell."

And he leans down, and I know...

This time...

He's going to kiss me.

His lips brush against mine, soft and sweet, and I breathe into his kiss, relief of I don't know what rushing through me.

The hand cupping my cheek dips into my hair, fingers twisting around strands of it as he pulls me in closer. The sweetness of the kiss dissolves, going hot, his tongue dipping between my lips. He swipes his tongue against mine, forceful and demanding, wanting more.

I melt into him, my breasts touching his naked chest, sending a thrill through me as my nipples respond, tightening against the warmth of his skin.

He pulls back. Sudden and cold. His hands go to my shoulders, pushing me away.

His hard gaze flashes over my face. What's he doing? Why the sudden change?

"Get dressed and meet me downstairs." He turns on his heel, leaving me, snapping up his shirt from beneath mine off the floor as he goes.

He tugs a knob on the wall and he's gone, leaving the door open behind him as he goes.

And finally, I let the tears fall.

What the hell just happened?

Liam

. . .

I STAND IN THE DOORWAY, SHOULDER LEANING ON THE DOORFRAME, arms crossed over my chest. Could have left by now but here I am. Why?

Fuck if I know.

I could lie to myself and say I'm observing her to see which brother she'd be the best match for. But I'm not.

And I don't make a habit of lying, to myself or anyone else. The truth is complicated enough.

I watch her as she shifts her weight on the seat of her wooden dining room chair, her nose crinkling as she tries to find relief from the plug.

It's fucking adorable.

Her lips are red and swollen from my kiss.

I look away.

The damn cat is still sitting by the door.

Marta comes bustling in from the kitchen, a plate of her home-made apple pie topped with vanilla ice cream and whipped cream in each hand.

Marta trying to fatten me up. My cue to leave. "Marta. Put her to bed for me."

"But I have pie for you." Marta sets Emilia's plate in front of her, and the other at the open seat right next to her.

"I'll pass." I'm walking through the door of the kitchen when I hear a murmured comment.

"Rude," Emilia says under her breath.

"What was that?"

"Someone offers you a plate of homemade pie and you turn it down? I thought you despised rudeness." She slices the prongs of her fork into the flaky pastry, popping a bite between those fuckable lips of hers. Her tongue pops out, lazily licking a drop of fresh whipped cream that's caught there. "Delicious."

I look from her to Marta's open, hopeful face, hovering by the table. "Fine."

Marta claps her hands then realizes what she's doing, snapping them back down, brushing her palms on her apron. She turns back to the kitchen. "Enjoy!"

I sink into the chair one seat over, sliding my plate across the table.

"Rude again."

Ignoring her, I stab an apple slice that's fallen from the crust. It's warm and gooey, a hint of cinnamon left on my tongue. Not bad.

"How's your ass feeling on that chair?" I ask, holding in a laugh.

She shakes her head, heaving a sigh. "I see my plan didn't work."

"What plan? You'd best not be plotting another escape." I stare out the back door. The damn cat stares back. "Or planning on bringing that cat inside."

She snorts. "So you can punish me again and put that gold monstrosity in my...? No. The pie." She nods at my empty plate. "It didn't sweeten you up like I'd hoped."

"There's no amount of sugar in this world that can make me sweet." I stand, nodding at the curve of her ass on the chair. "Take that thing out before bed."

Her eyes go wide as she shifts her weight, reminded of its presence. "By myself?"

"Yes."

"You're serious?" She pushes the end of her fork around her empty plate. "But... how?"

I watch the flush rise in her face. "You'll figure it out."

She's so innocent. The idea of removing the plug is causing her physical discomfort. She's folding her shoulders in, keeping her gaze from mine.

I slip a finger underneath her chin, forcing her eyes upward. "Are you not comfortable touching your own body? You haven't explored your perfect places with your pretty little fingers? I can teach you how." I love the pink blotches of shame blooming on her cheeks.

It leaves my balls tight, my cock aching.

Time for a visit to the Widow.

I need to rid myself of the sensual innocence of Emilia.

The Widow has experience, knows what she's doing.

It doesn't help that as I'm leaving, I catch a glimpse of Emilia, the naked virgin, standing bare breasted at her window, taunting me.

An hour later I'm satiated. I'm running on empty. Release flows through me, my limbs relaxing as I lie in the Widow's bed and light a smoke.

I'm completely fulfilled... so why does the thought of Emilia's lithe body, her hazy gray-green eyes, her little sneer...

Her innocence.... Her never-been-touched pussy waiting to be claimed...

It makes my cock stir beneath the Widow's sheets. Sheets that are still damp with our fucking.

The Widow takes a deep sip from her wine goblet, a brow raising at me. "You're thinking of her, aren't you?"

I don't answer the question. "I didn't touch her. I punished her, but I didn't... you know."

"Didn't what?" She gives a sultry laugh. "Fuck her?"

Her brash words make me pull back.

"Wow, boy scout. You didn't like that, did you? Your face went funny when you first told me about her. Now, you don't like me saying the word *fuck* when it comes to her." Her gaze narrows, her mind as always putting the pieces into place. "Don't tell me she's a virgin?"

"She'd better be if she's marrying one of us." I try to push aside the fact I just said one of us, instead of saying one of my brothers.

"Oh, shit." She stubs her cigarette out in her empty wineglass. "You've got to be kidding me."

"About what?"

"She's a fucking virgin. Supposedly going to one of your brothers. And here you are catching feels."

"No. I'm not."

"Could have fooled me," she says.

"No." I try to lower my voice. I've never been a man who had to raise it to get my point across. "I don't have feelings for her and besides, you know I don't do that shit."

"Do *that* shit?" She gives a throaty laugh. "You mean like dating and relationships and having meaningful connections with members of the opposite sex?"

I nod. "Yeah. That shit."

She gives a giggle. "You say it like it's hard drugs we're talking about instead of love."

Love? The word fills my stomach with unease.

My voice rumbles through the room. "What are you talking about? I've known this girl all of what? Five minutes? I punished her so she knows not to fuck with me and now I came here to clear my head and I'm going back home to figure out what to do with her."

"Clear your head?" She laughs again. "That's exactly what I'm talking about. You shouldn't have to clear your head of her. Unless…"

"Unless what?"

"Unless she's crawled under your skin." She taps a long finger against my skull. "She's gotten in your head."

She lights another cigarette, her little victory smoke for calling me out.

This girl is *not* allowed in my head. There's only one way to fix this.

I'm promising her to one of my brothers.

Tomorrow.

7

E*milia*

I'M STANDING IN MY BEAUTIFUL ROOM, MY ARMS WRAPPED AROUND MY
naked body. He watches me from the stone patio that surrounds
the pool. How I knew he'd be watching, I'm not sure, but there
he is.

I know he'll leave here soon. Go to his widow for relief. He could
have used me, had me over that pommel horse. I'm not even so sure
I would have objected, but he didn't.

I know it turned him on, punishing me. He's just as keyed up as I
am. He's left it to me to take this terrible plug out by myself, then
he'll go get his reward and I'm left with only my fumbling fingers.

Let me play my little game of power that I recently discovered,
taking him to the brink before he leaves to release the tension in
another woman's arms.

I stretch up my hands, lifting them above my head and hold onto the trim around either side of one of the large windows. I shake my hair over my shoulders, letting it swish in the moonlight. The nipples of my bare breasts graze the cold glass, rising into two hard peaks.

Begging to be kissed.

I stare down at him, my lips pouting into a smile.

He runs a hand over the back of his neck, his dark eyes glittering. I can almost hear his groans from where I stand in my second story window.

His gaze is hooked on me.

I blow him a kiss.

He reaches a hand up, lazily catches it, and slaps it onto the crotch of his pants.

Oh my God...

He turns and leaves.

It's okay, I tell myself, covering my breasts as I leave the window. I did what I set out to do. Made him want me.

It's only fair. The monster has me aching for him.

Naked, the moonlight streaming over my body as I move from the window, I go to pick up my clothing from the floor.

There's a light knock on the door. Who could that be? Hope rises in my heart that it's him but that'd be impossible. He was walking away from the house and there's no way he'd get up here that fast.

"Who is it," I ask, slipping into my leggings and top.

A woman's soft American voice calls through the door. "Hi there, it's Charlie. Liam sent me to... help you."

"Help me with the..."

"The plug." She gives a pretty laugh that relaxes me. "Yes."

Having another woman help me with such an intimate thing overwhelms me but I must be honest. I'm terrified of taking it out alone. He was right; I'm not comfortable touching my own body.

It's something he'd love to teach me, I'm sure.

I crack the door open, a flush rising in my cheeks before I even meet my savior. She's pretty. An open, friendly smile, long brown curls framing her face. She wears a floral dress and simple but elegant jewelry. A purse hangs at her hips.

I'd love a pair of the thin hoops she wears.

"I like your earrings," I say, holding the door open for her to come in.

She steps into the room, setting her bag on the armchair by the fire. "Thanks. I used to run the family jewelry store in New York, but when Liam was charged with establishing a branch of the family in Northern Italy, I begged him to let me tag along." She smiles and she's just so beautiful, I need to ask.

"Are you—with... Liam?" Is that jealousy in my tone?

She laughs again, the sound reminding me of the tinkling of silver bells at Christmas. "No. No. Nothing like that. He just needed a woman around to help run things. Marta takes care of the day to day, the food and cooking and cleaning, but there needed to be a Beauty around to make sure the place looks... Bachman."

I think of the beautiful, light, airy rooms I've been led to, my own gorgeous bedroom. Bachman taste is simple, timeless, elegant, and expensive. "You've done a wonderful job. I love my room."

"Thank you," she says.

Something she said stood out to me. "Did you say a 'Beauty' needed to be around?"

"Yes. It's just a nickname, what we women call ourselves. Any woman married to a man from the Bachman Brotherhood goes through a special ceremony on her wedding day, making her a member of the family and forever binding her to the other women in our group. She becomes a Beauty."

"Did your husband come with you?" I ask.

She shakes her head, curls swaying. "No." Are those tears welling in her eyes?

A feeling of unease comes over me. Have I struck a nerve? "Sorry. I, um—"

"No. it's fine. You couldn't have known. I started working at Bachman's Jeweler years ago. I just loved the family. I always hoped to be a part of it one day. Finally, I got my wish, married the man of my dreams."

One tear slips down her cheek. "I had the life I'd been fantasizing about for years. Unfortunately, it only lasted a few months. My husband died working one night, about two years ago. I've been a widow floating around ever since, still part of the family."

"Oh, I had no idea. I'm so sorry I asked," I say.

"It's okay. It's a wonderful, beautiful, luxurious life we Bachmans live, but it's not without its risks. I knew what I was getting into. But I couldn't stay at the Village anymore. I had to get away from there. Too many memories of my husband." She brushes the tear from her cheek and smiles. "When I found out Liam was moving to Italy, I begged him to let me come along. I'd seen photos of The Villa and fell in love. I knew I was supposed to come here to help him renovate."

I want to ask her a thousand questions, about her late husband, how they met, the family, the men, how they join the Brotherhood in the first place. I want to ask her if she'll remarry one day, if that's allowed, but I remember my manners and hold my tongue.

She points to the door of the massive, lavish, spa-like ensuite bathroom. "Ready?"

"Oh God," I say, moving toward the bathroom. "This is humiliating."

The plug feels heavy as I move. I'm dying to get rid of the thing.

"It's really not," she says. "It's the Bachman way. Don't think for a second I haven't been through everything you've been through tonight and more."

"More?" I squeak. Again, a thousand questions come to my mind, demanding answers, but I hold back.

I go to the bathroom counter, flipping on the lights. The white marble and tile room brightens, the teal sea glass tile backsplash shimmering in the illumination.

"I didn't do too bad in here, did I?" she says, her gaze admiring the room.

"Did you decorate it all?" I ask. I remember my father telling me the Bachmans had bought this estate about a year ago—The Villa they call it—complete with the main house, guest houses, pool house, pool, barn, and several other outbuildings. I can't imagine the money they must have to have renovated the entire ten-thousand-square-foot home, not to mention the guesthouse with the special attic room.

"Yes. We redid the entire house. Liam and his brothers had no clue what to do. If I'd left it up to them, the whole house would probably be fifty shades of gray."

"Sounds about right," I laugh, thinking of the rumors I've heard about the men in this family. "Speaking of," I say, my fingers wrapping around the counter. "How do I do this?"

"First of all?" She puts a soft hand on my shoulder. "Just relax."

I take a deep breath, my muscles squeezing against the plug. It reminds me of him. I think of his sexy, teasing grin as he planted the kiss I blew to him on his cock. And now, he's going to the widow. It's jealousy that I'm feeling creep its sticky fingers around my throat. I want the plug out. I don't want to think of him anymore tonight.

Shoving my shame aside, I tear off the leggings, kicking them along the tile floor. I stand there, staring in the mirror, my cropped shirt hovering above miles of bare skin.

Charlie's gaze catches my reflection. "It'll be alright. Everything works out in the end."

"If by *everything,* you mean an arranged marriage," I say.

Ignoring my comment, she moves behind me. "May I?"

I nod, tearing my gaze from the mirror. I bend at the waist, spreading my feet along the floor, widening the gap between my legs for her.

"Okay," she says, her fingers gently moving along my curves. "You grab the stem of the plug and start pulling gently." Her fingers press between my cheeks as she grabs the handle of the plug. "Do you want to try?"

"No thanks." I squeeze my eyes shut tight, shaking my head, my palms going damp against the counter. "Please, you do it."

"So, when he put it in you, the narrowest part went in first. But when you're taking it out, the widest part has to come out first." She gives it a tug and my ass unwillingly clenches around the plug like it wants to keep it in. "Feel that? Your muscles tighten around it when you are trying to take it out. You go slow and gentle."

"Thank God he sent you to help. I had no idea what I was doing." The question hangs over my head and this one, I allow myself to ask. "Why didn't he do it himself?"

She shakes her head. "Liam is... complicated. I can't pretend to know what goes on in his mind. But I have a feeling..." Her words trail off like she's saying too much.

I turn to look over my shoulder, catching her eye. This is so intimate, with her so close to my naked body, her fingers slowly pulling the plug from my ass. Why can't she tell me?

"Push a little," she says, tugging on the plug.

"God. This is humiliating." I can't believe I'm letting this woman, this stranger, remove the plug. But I'm desperate and Charlie has a soothing presence. I like her. I bear down as she tugs on the plug and it works, we have some movement, the thing slowly exiting my body.

I hate him for putting this thing in me. I hate him for sending her. I hate him for not being here to do this himself.

I ask again. "Why is he not here?"

"Because," she says. The widest part of the plug is out and the rest slips out easily. It leaves me feeling vacant and empty, my muscles contracting but finding nothing there. "He's afraid to let himself feel something for you."

She moves around me, going to the sink to clean the thing.

He feels something for me. "Oh my God," I say, grabbing for the plug. "I can do that. You don't have to." I take it from her, washing it with soapy fingers and rinsing it well under the tap. I leave it resting on a soft towel on the counter.

I'm ready for a shower.

Charlie gives me a naughty grin. "I brought you something. Every woman, especially one tied to a Bachman man, should know her own body. How to bring herself pleasure. This is a bare-it-all-to-your-man kind of world and you'll find way more enjoyment if you're comfortable with yourself. Wait here."

I slip my leggings back on, washing my hands again.

She comes back into the bathroom, purse strap on her shoulder. Looking down, she rifles through her purse, pulling out a sleek black box.

"Here," she says, placing the box in my hands. "Take your time. Play with it. See what you like."

"Um... okay. Thanks?" The box is light. What could it hold?

"Look, Emilia. You're going to be okay. I promise. And if you have any questions while you're here, I want you to know you can come to me."

"Thanks, Charlie."

She gives me a smile like she wants to say something else, then purses her lips, leaving me with a nod.

Only when the bedroom door closes am I brave enough to pull off the lid.

"Oh my God!" Heat flushes my face as I pull out the first item. It's a vibrator, that I'm sure of, its cock-like silicone shape a deep purple, a gold band running around the bottom, offering different settings. But stemming from the center of the shaft is a teardrop-shaped appendage, narrow at the top, growing wider at the bottom. Just like the plug. "Is this thing meant to go in two places at once?"

I twirl it in my hands, too shy to turn it on. In the black velvet-lined depths of the box is a tube of jelly. Below that is another toy. This one fits perfectly in my palm, its shape like a face buffer I have at home only instead of a pad for cleaning skin, there's a small white doughnut-shaped thing at the top, its center cavity empty. "Is that for..." I read the words on the handle. *Just for Her Clitoral Stimulation.*

Now my face is a hundred degrees. I drop the toys in the box, tossing the lid on and go for a ridiculously long, cool shower. As the water streams over my heated skin, rinsing the lavender-scented soap I've scrubbed every inch of my body with, I think of the words of advice Charlie left me with.

A woman should know her own body. I think of the toys, curiosity peaking. I dry my skin with one of the fluffy white towels that have been left for me.

I wander to the wardrobe at the far end of the room. The house was built in the early 1900's and they've not added closets to this room. I open its doors. As I suspected, it's full of clothing and shoes, everything in my size. When did he have time to do this? I take my time, fingering the delicate material of the gowns, feeling the weight of the expensive shoes in my hands.

I open the drawers of the dresser, finding what I'm searching for.

There's a short, black, skimpy nightgown, edged in lace. I pull it from the drawer, slipping it over my head. The fabric is cool and slippery against my skin. I feel... sexy. I catch a glimpse of myself in the mirror and the heat in my cheeks is working for me. I look pretty. Ready to take a moment and get to know myself.

I light candles, placing them on various flat surfaces in the room, the dresser, the mantel. I flick the gas logs on and a moment later, they come to life, filling the dark room with a warm glow. The soft scent of jasmine floats through the air.

I go to the bed, folding back the fluffy white comforter. I lie down in the center of the bed, my nightgown slipping along the cotton sheets.

Nestled in the pillow, I grab the black box from where I put it on the nightstand. I take off the lid, curiosity laced with shame filling me.

Uncomfortable with touching my body, I snap open the lid of the jelly, smoothing it over both tips of the vibrator. I go to wipe the excess jelly from my fingers onto my thigh when I pause. What the hell? I might as well do as Charlie said.

With visions of his fingers on me instead of my own, I move my slick fingers to my sex, slowly dipping them inside my tight entrance. It feels good, but every part of me wishes it was him touching me. Which disgusts me.

What's wrong with me? Lusting after my captor.

I slip my fingers from my sex, ignoring my ass. I can't take it that far.

"Here we go." I turn the vibrator to the lowest setting and slip it between my thighs. "Oh my God."

Just the hum of the toy against my thigh has a wave of arousal flowing. Didn't even need the jelly, did I? I try to relax, closing my eyes, but the only thing that makes the experience pleasurable is...

Thinking of him.

Ugh.

Still, I move the pulsing head of the toy to the entrance of my sex, surprised by the sharp whine that rises in the back of my throat upon contact. I've only ever had his fingers inside me and the toy is slender, but still, I'm tight and my sex stretches as I push the toy inside of me.

I want it to be *him* filling my sex, not the toy, but still. My God, it feels good. I push the vibrator inside me further, surprised when the very tip of the other limb finds my asshole, pressing against it.

Another whine fills me, but I can't stop. Release is so close and after the plug, my ass is begging for the silicone nub to be inside. I push it in further, letting the nub enter my ass as the main part of the vibrator goes deeper inside me.

The result is the world's most intense orgasm hitting me hard and fast, my eyes squeezing shut, a tight white burst of light flashing from behind my lids, and I see his face. "Oh my God," I whisper, my body curling in on itself as the climax tears through me, leaving me shuddering. A second orgasm starts to build and I quickly switch the thing off, unable to take more.

I toss the thing on the bed beside me, pulling the covers up and over me as I collapse back onto the pillows. "What was that?"

My fingers dig into the comforter, my toes still curled.

There's a knock on my door. Oh shit! Is it him? I look down, making sure the box and toys are hidden under the fluffy covers.

I try to smooth the strain from my voice. "Come in?"

He walks in, smelling of clean, musky cologne and a faint hint of cigarette smoke. A pang rips through my heart at the sight of his wild hair, mussed from her hands, his mussed clothing, wrinkled from being torn from his body and tossed to the floor. He's been with his widow. That's for sure.

Charlie's words swell in my mind at the sight of him... *He's afraid to let himself feel something for you.*

His face looks pained, discomfort flashing in his gaze as he takes me in, black silk against white cotton. "I don't apologize. But I will say, I probably should have been here." Does he mean instead of at his booty call with the widow, he should have been here to take the plug out of me? "I should have been here to help you."

I need him to leave, the vibrator suddenly feeling like a big, purple elephant under my covers. "It's fine. Really. Don't worry about it. I think I just need to sleep." I throw in a stretch and a yawn for dramatic effect.

He doesn't take his eyes from me. It appears as if just looking at me is causing him physical pain. I lower my stretched arms, letting the thin lace strap of the gown slide down my shoulder.

He swallows. Hard. Reaching in his pocket, he pulls something out. He slips a red leather jewelry box onto the nightstand. "This is for you. A gift."

I cock a brow at him. "You mean, an *apology* gift?"

"I told you. I don't apologize." He leaves the box on the nightstand, giving me one longing look. "Sleep well."

He has no idea how well I'll sleep, relaxation from the afterglow of the toy finally seeping through my muscles.

He looks like he wants to take a seat on the edge of the bed. I imagine my vibrator coming to life under his ass. What would he think of that?

Please, no... Just go!

He thinks better of it, leaving me without a backward glance.

"Goodnight!" I call to the closed door.

I lift the box from the nightstand, the leather cool against my skin, snapping open the lid. Nestled in black velvet sits a pair of thin hoops, gold to Charlie's silver ones I'd admired earlier tonight. I lift one from the box, eager to try it on. I go to the mirror, putting on the earrings. The hoops are large enough they swing as I move.

"They're gorgeous." I stare at my reflection, thinking I look older with the earrings on.

I love them. I love that he somehow found out I liked Charlie's and had a pair for me only hours later. With his extravagant giftand my experience tonight, I no longer feel so much like the virgin girl that I am. I'm beginning to feel like... a woman.

I dive back under the covers, greedy to experiment with my gifts.

8

L *iam*

Marta hands me my morning espresso. "Thank you."

"You're very welcome." She's got a smug little smile on her face.

"What?"

I take a sip. Hot and rich. Like me and the boys.

God, what's gotten into me? I've got bachelors on the brain today.

"Nothing." She gives an innocent shrug. "You just look... well rested."

"Thank you." I give her a nod, dismissing her.

She dashes off, practically giggling and trying to hide it.

She thinks I've got a thing for the girl. I can read it on her face. She's dead wrong. I'm relaxed because I was with the Widow last night. Not the girl.

Speaking of Emilia... where is she?

I find her in the walled garden, kneeling in the grass. She's wearing her uniform of black leggings and a white tee. She's got the gold hoops in her ears, the sneakers that I bought her on her feet. I'm glad she likes the gifts. Seeing her wear them makes me lean into my relaxation a little more.

I like having her here.

She's bent over the bushes, cooing at something rustling in the leaves. Must be that damn cat again.

I move closer, kneeling beside her. "He's not coming in the house."

So enamored with her new plaything, she barely acknowledges my existence. "Come, come, little one. I won't hurt you."

There's more rustling as whatever it is she's chasing moves further back toward the stone wall.

"Don't be scared." Finally, she looks over at me. "Oh, I see. Yes. I'd be scared too if this big old man was looming over me."

"Am I that bad?"

She gives me an exasperated look. "Can you please go away? I'm trying to get the monkey out of the bushes."

"Monkey? Oh, God. Not that flea-infested thing." I groan, remembering Po's terrible idea to impress a girl he was talking to. A gift of a pet monkey. The monkey hated her, she gave it back to him, Po took that as a bad sign, and broke it off. "I guess Marta's been feeding him."

"Him? What's his name?" She turns back to the bush, making little whispering sounds. "Do you have any food on you?"

"Me?" I look down at my Armani suit. Casual, but still... no place for a packet of peanuts. "Do I look like the kind of man wandering around with snacks in my pockets?"

Her gaze stays intent on the bushes. "Well, can you go get me something? Crackers or cookies, maybe? Wait. Are they supposed to have sugar?"

My tone is stern. "No crackers. No cookies. No cats. No monkeys."

"Aww." She looks up at me with wide eyes and a pout. "Does the grumpy man hate animals and sugar? You're missing out. They both bring so much joy to life. I mean, have you even had one of Marta's cinnamon rolls? I had one this morning with extra frosting *and* a caramel latte. Yum."

There's more noise from the leaves. We watch as the tiny tan monkey dashes out of the bushes, running along the wall.

"Darn." She plops down on her ass, crossing her legs. "You scared him off. Now I'm never going to get him to come inside."

"Come inside? There's no way in hell—"

She puts a hand over mine. "Joking." She looks up at me, her gray-green eyes sparkling with teasing.

Her eyes are so pretty. Why am I staring? I clear my throat, glancing down at her hand on mine. "Oh. Well, then. Um. Good."

She takes her hand away, leaving my skin feeling cold in its absence.

"Well, I'd better go get ready. I've got a husband to catch. Don't I?" She stands, brushing off the seat of her leggings, and leaves me kneeling in the garden. I watch her walk the entire way to the house, enjoying every step. She has the grace and beauty of a queen.

The door closes and I'm left alone in the garden, thinking of her. Only, I'm not alone. Am I?

I look over my shoulder. A loud meow rises from the other side of the bushes. "You've got to be kidding me."

The tomcat comes sidling out of the greenery, giving me an ornery look. I give one right back. "What are you looking at? Get the hell out of here."

He hisses, then lifts a paw to his lips and licks it, daring me to touch him.

"Fine. Just know the only way you come into that house," I point at our beautiful estate home, clean and unmarred by pets, "is stuffed."

I leave the gardens. I've got wilder things to tame than wild animals.

Single. Brothers.

Seven unmarried men sit at the long dining room table. Some of the men here today are brothers by blood: Cannon, Tristan, Hunter, Dom. Others have come to be as close to me as my blood brothers: Enzo, Leo, and Po. All are my brothers by the code of the Bachman Brotherhood.

Emilia will sit at the head, surrounded by their attentions. A smile tugs at my lips. She's probably going to hate this.

Speed dating.

Widow Russo told me about it. She's put herself back on the market. Apparently, our emotionless meetings no longer satisfy her. She's on different apps and internet dating sites, but she said the most brutal—and best—way to find a match is these mini sessions where you rotate from stranger to stranger, spending a few minutes with each. You answer questions and see if there's any chemistry.

Only I'm going to let them all have at her at once. Let her get flustered. I'll see which man is best suited to handle her.

I'm not expecting her to come down those stairs looking like she does. I was anticipating the bike shorts and crop top I always seem to visualize when I think of her, her hair pulled back in a youthful ponytail, her face bare of makeup.

A girl.

She's not that at all.

As her manicured blood-red fingernails slide down the curving wooden banister, she catches my eye. Sexy Emilia has come out to play. And she wants to beat me at my own game.

Her hair flows over her shoulders in loose curls. Her eyes are lined with black kohl, her lashes impossibly thick and long. She glossed her lips, accentuating the fullness of her pout.

She found the floor-length red silk gown, the sleeveless one with the slit cut high to her mid-thigh.

The dress was meant for a ball or a dinner with the entire family.

Not for a simple Saturday morning at the table with my brothers. A long, toned leg slips out from between the skirt as she moves down the stairs, elegant and sure of herself. She breezes by me, a cloud of heady perfume in her wake.

"What," she asks, eyeing the table filled with handsome men, "is going on here? All these gorgeous men for me?"

She passes by them, looking them over one by one. Dom, usually shy, now the most eager to please, rises from his chair, holding hers out. "Here. Sit with us." He offers her an easy smile.

"Thank you." She smiles back but her gaze travels back to mine.

Taking stock of my emotions? Seeing if I'll be jealous? Unclear.

She slides into the seat, folding her hands on top of the table like a queen. I've never met her mother; she passed away long before I moved here, but I've heard she was beautiful and self-assured. I wonder if Emilia resembles her now.

"I brought you here to get to know some of my brothers," I say.

"Some?" Her brows rise. "And I thought my four was a lot. Your mother must have been a very busy woman."

Light laughter travels through the room.

I clear my throat, ready to begin. "You met them the other night, all but Cannon." Cannon does a half stand, greeting her with vague disinterest and a wordless nod. He is married to his club and wants to keep it that way. "And each of them needs a wife."

A flash of naked fear dances in her eyes.

She blinks it away. "Well, I've been told I need a husband. Should we get to know one another better, boys?" She leans forward, pressing her breasts together in the most appealing way.

Fuck.

What happened to the innocent wallflower who shook in my presence? This is a woman, ready to meet her fate head-on.

"I like the looks of all of you." She offers an all-too-suggestive grin, eyeing the men.

Fuck. Fuck. Fuck.

Jealousy rips through me, hot and true. I can't shake it off. Po leans in. "What would you like to know?" He sends her a friendly, open grin.

Po is likeable. Easy. Funny.

A man that would set her at ease. I always seem to put her on edge.

"Oh, my first victim." She giggles. "I mean, volunteer, of course."

Again, the men laugh, their eyes glued to her.

"Tell me," she says. "What do you all have to do to join the Brother-hood? Is there like an initiation or something?"

The table goes quiet. She raises her brow. "Oops. Was that the wrong question?"

After being chosen and vetted, we do go through a terrible, grueling initiation process to join. Not all who try make it through, but those who prove their strength, determination, and grit get the ultimate reward. Becoming Bachman. But the initiation is an abso-lute secret and we do not speak of it outside the Brotherhood, not even with our wives.

Po smooths over the moment. "Let's talk about something more interesting. How you would become a Beauty. Would that be alright?"

"I'll allow it." She smiles back at him. I can't tell if there's real chem-istry there or if she's playing with me. But there it is—her gaze sliding back to mine, looking for a reaction.

"When a woman marries a Bachman, she becomes a Beauty." He opens his hands, spreading his arms out before him. "And the whole world is opened to her. Traveling, shopping, dining, anything she wants, really, she gets. What's ours is hers and she'll never want for anything."

Emilia cocks a brow at him, the grin falling from her face. "Except her freedom."

There're a few uncomfortable laughs.

"True." Po keeps the smile on his face, leaning closer to her. Jeal-ousy rages inside my chest as Po inches even closer. "Once a Bach-man, always a Bachman. You can never leave. But. The way we care for our women?" He shakes his head. "I've never heard of a woman wanting to leave."

She runs the tip of her tongue over her lips. "Is that so?"

"Yes." He lifts his hand as if to put it over hers. I'm over to her in a matter of a half-second, my hand pulling hers out from under his before he can touch her. I'd hate to have to break his fingers. He's incredible with a rifle.

"Excuse us for a minute." I grab Emilia by her hand and pull her from her seat.

She rises with a surprised, "Ooh!" I feel the men watching us as we leave.

"Where are you taking me?" She tugs at my hand.

I don't answer her, pulling her into the small workroom off the big kitchen. There's a round table here with two chairs, for staff to take a break. I set her down in a chair, slamming down in the one opposite of her.

"Let's play our own little get-to-know-you game," I say, slapping my palms flat on the tabletop.

She jumps, giving me a look like she wants to slap me or kiss me. I'm not sure which and I don't care.

I stare her down. "Tell me why you are wearing that dress of all the dresses we bought for you. Why the sexiest one?"

"I'm trying to impress my potential husbands." She shrugs. "Don't you like it? You picked it out."

"*Who* are you wearing it for?" My gaze burns into hers.

She leans forward, dropping one word on the table between us. "Me."

"Fair enough." I lean back, wishing she'd said she wore it for me. My mind's eye goes back to last night when I brought her the earrings and found her lying in bed alone, wearing that sexy black nightgown. "But who were you thinking of last night, lying all alone in that bed, wearing the black silk nightie I bought you. Who were you thinking of then?"

Her eyes hold mine. "Who were you thinking of last night, while I was lying in that bed all alone, in the black silk nightie you bought me?" Her brows rise slowly. "Your widow?"

So, she knows about my visits to Widow Russo. And... she cares. They bother her.

She wore the dress for me. She thinks of me. Often.

I tell her the truth, tired of the half-lies of denial I've been feeding myself.

We sit at the small kitchen table, facing one another, both thinking of last night.

"You." I hold her gaze. "Last night, I was thinking of you. When my cock was buried deep inside of *her,* I was wondering what it would feel like to be inside of you. I wondered what you were doing back at The Villa while I was at the Widow's house. I thought of you, of your naïveté, your innocence, all set off by your toughness, and I thought of your body the entire time I was with her." I press my hands into the wood, leaning closer. "Is that what you wanted to hear?"

Her teeth sink into her bottom lip, her head shaking. Her eyes go shiny with unshed tears. "No."

"No?" I sound like a damn parrot. "No?"

"No. I'd rather hear you weren't thinking those things. Because I was thinking about you, when I was alone in my bed. I tried to fight it but there you were, your face in my mind, your hands on my body. You were there, even though I was alone, and I never, ever want to let a man get a hold on me like that."

My voice is thick. "And that would be easier to do if I wasn't also thinking of you?" I ask.

She nods.

"Shit." I rub a hand over the back of my neck.

She wants me. I want her. Where do we go from here?

I can't tear my gaze away from hers.

Po comes to the doorway. "Hey, Liam."

I answer him, still looking at her. "Not now."

They know not to interrupt me but Po presses on. "We've got company. Emilia's father. He's here. And so are her brothers."

At the mention of her family, Emilia's face goes ashen.

I leave the table, Emilia hot on my heels. Her father stands in the entryway. Antonio, the eldest and most vicious from what I've heard, stands at his father's side, green eyes flashing at me. Her other three burly brothers stand behind them.

Her father reaches his arms out to his daughter. "Emilia. Darling. Look how beautiful you are."

"Dad." Emilia goes to him, letting him embrace her in a stiff hug. "What are you doing here?"

Her brothers cross their arms over their chests almost in unison as her father speaks.

"We've come to take you home, dear." He looks at me.

He's making a play. Emilia is his pawn.

Her brow furrows. "What do you mean?"

"We've found a higher bidder." The head of the Accardi family grins, his face oozing with confidence.

She goes rigid in his arms. Her gaze finds mine. "What?"

Something in her eyes tears through me, making me want to protect her from her father and beg her to stay.

Her father says, "Yes, dear Emilia."

But when he says her name, it comes out sounding like Emily.

Emily. Emily. Emily.

The name sends me spiraling down a cold shaft, my mind going black, my limbs numb.

Once.

I made the mistake once before.

Of letting a girl steal my heart right out of my chest. She shattered it. Destroyed me. Left me in slivers impossible to ever be fully put back together.

I can't do an Emily again. I won't survive.

I don't make the same mistake twice.

I can't have Emilia for myself.

If I can't have her, I can't let one of my brothers marry her.

That whole "don't covet your brother's wife" rule.

She'd be the bane of my existence. It'd be torture, having to see her every day with someone else. Never being allowed to touch her.

Forget this alliance. There're other families. There are other girls.

Her father's greed has saved me.

"Take her," I say, crossing the room to her father. I move in close, so my face is a beat away from his. "But if you ever raise a hand to her again, I'll end you."

I watch his gaze to be sure I see what I need to see. Fear. He gives me a nod of submission, looking away with a sheepish gaze.

I leave the room without giving her a backward glance.

I can't look at her. Cracks lead to shatters.

9

E *milia*

MY GAZE WANDERS AROUND THE PEELING WALLPAPER OF MY OLD room, unable to believe that just hours ago, I was taking a luxurious bubble bath in my private spa at the Bachman estate. Choosing from hundreds of beautiful outfits. Smoothing on lotions so expensive it felt like rubbing silk over my skin, applying expensive makeup to my face, perfume behind my ears.

I had friends. Marta... Charlie... Even *he* was starting to feel like a... I don't know.

Sitting across from him at that kitchen table, admitting to each other that we think of one another... often, I could no longer deny to myself that I have feelings for him.

Now, I collapse on my rumpled bedcovers, my dress wrinkling. My makeup is surely smudging around my eyes, dark shadows making tracks down my cheeks from the tears running down my face. I go to my bathroom, dampen a washcloth, and wash the makeup from my face.

The girl staring back at me in the mirror is a shell of herself. I was ripped from my budding Bachman life, dumped back into the archaic Accardis. How could he do this to me?

And how did I fall for the Bachmans so quickly? For him? Was my loyalty to my family so easily bought? Torn away with a room full of clothing and one visit to his mysterious, thrilling attic room?

No. I shake my head. I'm not easily bought by things.

It was *him* that made me want to stay.

I'm so confused. I wish I had a woman to talk to. Marta or Charlie. They'd help me sort out these emotions.

Instead, I'm trapped in a house full of dumb boys.

There's a knock on my door. "Go away!" I fold the washcloth, leaving it on the counter. I flop back down on my bed.

Just like I knew would happen, there's a clinking in the lock, the door thrown wide open. They keep a pin above the doorframe for whenever I attempt to lock myself in. Antonio slides into my room.

"Go away," I say again, but the look in his eyes makes me shrink back to the furthest corner of my bed. He likes what he sees. Too much. Staring at me way longer than a brother should a sister. "Please. Go away."

It feels as if his green eyes are peeling the dress from my body. "I will. But not until I've touched that dress."

My stomach goes sour, flip-flopping in my belly. "Antonio. Don't."

I inch back, pressing my shoulders into the wall. I gather up the covers, trying to hide my body, the one I so desperately wanted Liam to admire, but now wish every inch was covered. I feel sick.

"Who were you wearing that dress for? One of them? All of them?" He reaches out, grabbing an end of a curl and tugging it. "Our little bird turned into a peacock."

"Stop."

He leans in closer, his fingertip running over the silky neckline of the dress. "Which one were you hoping to fuck? Or was it all of them at once? Did you visit their club?" His finger leaves the dress, dipping down between my breasts.

"I said stop!" I grab his finger, pull it out of my dress, and bend it back. Hard.

Shock and pain flash through his gaze as he pulls his hand from mine. "Fuck!"

Fear eases out of me, replaced by anger. "Touch me again, and I'll break it next time."

I stare at him until he backs away from me.

"Jesus, Em. Can't you take a joke?" Something in my face keeps him from approaching me again. A sick calm runs through me, knowing I've gained a bit of power.

"I could if you were funny. You're not. Get out of my room."

His face twists into a mask of revenge. "I came here to tell you something. Don't you want to hear it?"

"What?"

"Your fiancée is here. Downstairs. He can't wait to meet you." Antonio gives me a devil's grin. He smiles like he's got a terrible secret. One he's going to love to watch and I'm going to hate. Antonio straightens his spine, holding out an arm to me. "Come on down. Let big brother escort you."

I push back the covers, which slide away from the dress. I leave my feet bare. I take the arm he offers me, not because I want to, but because my knees are suddenly so weak, I can barely stand.

I'm about to meet the stranger I'll spend the rest of my life with.

Antonio leads me down the stairs. "Seriously. You could do better."

"Thanks a lot."

He takes me to the library. My father and another man his age sit in the worn wingback chairs by the cold fireplace. I look around for the man's son, the man I'm supposed to marry.

There's no one else in this room.

Where is his son?

I glance at my brother. I can't tell if he's smiling or scowling but he stares at the man beside my father. "This is John Romano, and he's asked for your hand in marriage."

I take a closer look at the man. He's older than my father by at least ten years, making him three times my age...

"No way." The words come from me whispered and harsh. "You're too old to be—"

My father snaps, "Emilia! Manners! Our family is extremely fortunate to be accepting a proposal from the Romano family."

I think of John Romano's handsome sons, Luca and Lance, and their beautiful brides. I'm younger than all of them.

John stands, offering me a smile and a cool hand. "Emilia. I remember you from your christening."

My stomach turns as I accept his hand. My christening? The age gap between us shows itself, heady and loud, blaring at me with its monstrosity till I can barely breathe.

"Hello," I say, remembering my manners. I accept his hand. "I apologize for my outburst. I was just surprised... that's all."

He pats my hand as a grandfather would a granddaughter. "I understand. It's not every day a bride meets her groom."

My guts wrench. I'm going to be sick. "If you'll excuse me just a moment. All the excitement... I'm feeling a bit faint."

"Of course. I've waited years to be ready to take on a wife. What's another day?"

"D—day?" I say, my voice shaky.

"That's right." My dad holds my gaze, daring me to defy him. "Mr. Romano was so eager when we agreed to his proposal, he set the date right on the spot. Tomorrow."

"Tomorrow..."

Now I really am going to be sick. I turn from the room, flying down the hall and up the stairs.

I hear Antonio's smooth voice behind me. "Women. So emotional. Don't worry, she'll be ready when you arrive in the morning."

I lie in my bed, crying. Why did I let myself feel something for Liam? He's a monster, just like I first thought on that road. He made me want him, then sent me back here to be married to someone else.

I hate men. All men.

I never, ever want to marry.

I tried to be loyal to my family, to swallow the thought of an arranged marriage to help them. But I... can't. Not after falling for the Bachman life, then seeing that man downstairs, old enough to be my grandfather. I can't have Liam, and I don't want anyone else.

For once in my life I want to do something just for me.

Run away, far away from here.

But I have no money, no friends, no protection.

I'm utterly, desperately lost.

What can I do?

LIAM

I MUST HAVE SOME RELEASE. I'M LOSING MY MIND. I CAN ONLY THINK of her and him, whoever he is. The thought of whoever she's been promised to, his hands on her...

I bang on the Widow's front door. In my haste to get away from my own home, I've come unannounced.

She opens the door just as I'm about to beat on it with my fist. She holds it open a crack, her lovely face poking through.

"Liam. What are you doing here? I have guests." She glances over her shoulder, calling to her visitors, "Just a minute, I'll be right there!"

I run a hand over the back of my neck, desperate for the relief she can give me. "Please. I just need a few minutes with you."

"You mean your cock needs a few minutes inside of me?" she laughs.

"Exactly," I say.

"I'm sorry," she whispers through the crack in her door. "I was going to call you tomorrow and tell you but since you're here on my doorstep, I'll just tell you now."

"Tell me what?" I grab the frame of her door in my hand, leaning toward her. The sound of laughing voices and the clinking of glasses float toward me. "Who's here?"

"I told you. I have guests," she says. She shakes her head. "I can't see you anymore. I've met someone and he gave me an ultimatum. No more men on the side."

"Met someone..." Her internet dating... I didn't think about what would happen if it worked. I had no idea she was looking for a serious partner. "Who?"

She rolls her eyes knowing I'll object to who she's about to say. "Roberto Casamino."

"Roberto." The man that runs the hardware store. Boring. Predictable. Safe. "That guy?"

But I can see it. After the intensity of her last husband, the deep love she felt for him, the danger his line of work brought into her life, his death, her loss, she just wants someone soft, someone she can count on. Companionship.

I'm happy for her, but I foresee her boredom in their bedroom. I smile, offering a farewell to a good friend. "You're always welcome to call me if you need a good fuck."

"It's not me you really want, anyway," she says, looking away.

"What do you mean?" I ask.

Her eyes lock on mine. "It's not me you want."

"I..." What does she want me to say? She knows, doesn't she? That the last few times we've been together... it wasn't her I was imagining.

The words slip out. "I'm sorry." The words are simple but freeing. Has Emilia changed my heart so much I'm now... apologizing?

"It's fine." She gives a shake of her head. "Besides... I don't think you'll be available much longer."

She's speaking of Emilia.

I shake my head. "You're wrong."

"Am I? I see the way you look whenever her name comes up—"

"She's gone." I lean over, my gut feeling as if it's been punched. When I speak, my voice is tight but controlled. "Her father found a higher bidder. She's marrying another man."

"Is that so..." She bites her lip, looking off into the distance, past me. "Do you know who?"

I shake my head. "I didn't ask."

"Liam," she says, her brow narrowing in thought. "It's the strangest thing. Bob and I were invited to John Romano's wedding. But the whole thing seemed so weird, very rushed, I only just found out about it today. Could he be marrying Emilia?"

John Romano heads one of the families I need an alliance with, but he has no daughters to marry. He's older, at least twice Emilia's age. A decent man, but to think of his grandfatherly hands on her young body, I see red.

It can't be.

I think of the way the Accardis burst into my home. They were rushed, like they'd just gotten the good news of a higher offer. "When is the wedding?"

"Tomorrow." Her eyes hold mine. "John Romano is getting married tomorrow morning."

10

L *iam*

THERE. SHE'S THERE IN THE WINDOW, STILL WEARING MY RED DRESS.
Her knees are curled up against her chest, her arms wrapped
around them. She's... crying.

Fuck.

It hurts me and my chest heaves, physical pain shooting through
me at the sight of her tears.

Therefore, I should let her go. She makes me weak.

Another man has claimed her and unless I want to start a war, I
have to let her marry.

I don't know what I'm doing, but now I'm grabbing the edge of the
first-floor roofing, pulling myself up and over onto the roof. Her
room has a little balcony off it. I stretch up, lift my legs, and get a
footing on the outer edge of the balcony with the toe of my boot.

Shimmying my hands further up, I stand, holding onto the edge of the railing.

She makes me weak and yet, pulling myself over her balcony railing, being this close to her, I feel stronger than I have in years. One foot up to the top of the railing and crouched like a panther, I spring over, landing with soft feet in the center of the balcony. I go to the glass door and slide it open.

She startles as the door opens. I put a finger to my lips. When she sees my face, the tears dry, a smile coming, then quickly fading.

She leaps from the bed, rushing over to me, whisper-hissing, "What are you doing here?"

"I don't know," I say, pulling her face toward me with my hands.

Her gaze is a mixture of hatred and longing. She doesn't know whether to kiss me or slap me. I make the decision for both of us. I press my lips against hers, take her with my tongue, claiming her mouth.

My hand searches her body, gliding over all the perfect places I wanted to touch the first moment I saw her in this dress. Palms against silk, I caress the perfection that is her body. I run my fingers over the neckline of her dress, wanting to dip my fingers underneath to her breasts.

She captures my fingers in her hand, pulling them away from her neckline.

"What?" I ask.

She shakes her head. "It's nothing."

I kiss her again, running both my hands over her ass, cupping and squeezing her there. She likes that, purring into our kiss and melting into me.

Why am I kissing her? My hand winds into her hair, tangling in her long locks, holding her to me so I can run my tongue deeper into her mouth. Why am I here?

I want her.

"I want to have you. For all of eternity, I want to be the man who had you first."

"That's why you came?" Her eyes narrow. She pulls away, shaking her head. "No. Absolutely not."

"Maybe I'm not asking." My blood heats, my hands growing greedier. I can't pull myself away from her. I don't want to.

She pushes a feeble hand against my chest. "How could you send me back here?" Tears brim in her eyes once more. It makes my heart break.

"I'm sorry." I look down, shaking my head with my apology. "I can't marry you. And I couldn't let one of my brothers marry you. I would have killed them, seeing one of them with you."

"You can't marry me..." Her words trail off.

Is that a question? How do I tell her my heart is a broken thing, incapable of love? That I can't endure the pain of losing someone else? "You deserve a man who... wants a marriage. I don't."

"Fair enough." She looks away.

I don't know what to say. I just want to kiss her.

"You don't know what it's like... here." Her voice cracks. She shakes her head, blinking back tears. She steels her nerves, straightening her spine. "I don't want to marry Romano. But to get what you want, you'll have to do something for me."

Her eyes find mine, challenging me.

"What are you saying? What do you want?" I bring my hands up high, dipping them into her panties. I find her entrance, filling her with two of my fingers.

She gives a gasp, the back of her head falling against the wall. She cups her hand over mine. "Please," she begs.

What does she beg for? More of my touches? Marriage? Love? Things I can't give her?

I breathe into her ear, "What do you want?" On my inhale I take in her heady scent. Vanilla and honey and ripe womanhood, begging to be plucked.

She shakes her head, grabbing my gaze. Her eyes hold that steely determination I remember from that day in my office, the expression that made my pen, hovering over the *no* column, move to the *yes*.

"Please. Take me away from here. I *never* want to marry," she says. "Ever. To any man. I want you to take me far away. Give me that, and I'll give you what you want. Right now." She reaches up a hand, brushing my cheek with soft fingers.

"You're going to start a war, little girl." I crook my fingers inside her, stroking her clit with the pad of my thumb.

"Not necessarily," she says through shaky breaths. "When they come to get me tomorrow, all they'll know is I'm not here. I could have run off on my own. Take me somewhere and give us time to sort this out. I just know—I can't marry him."

I kiss her as I touch her, biting kisses that leave a trail of marks along her neck.

"Ruin me. Take me and make me unmarriable. Then, take me away from this place. I never want to see it again. Ruin me." She closes her eyes. "Ruin me."

11

E *milia*

"Ruin me," I say again. My eyes close, my head leaning against the wall and as his fingers slide in and out of me, I realize...

He already has.

I want him when I should hate him. He's the monster who stole me from my home, then sent me back. He flicks his thumb over my clit, sending shockwaves through my body, and I think of the brothers at his table. A few were funny, kind. Normal enough. And I wanted nothing to do with any of them.

So many handsome, available men and I couldn't take my eyes off... *him.*

Something about the way he is holds so much of what I crave. Blame my violent upbringing, the rough edges that came with love, but his touch is what I need. His hands slide up my neck, caressing where he's bruised my skin with his biting kisses.

Marking me as his. Mark away. Anything to keep me from marrying.

He doesn't want a wedding either. Maybe we can keep this up, play this game, fulfill one another without having to put a name on what this is between us. I had an IUD put in when my father first started this arranged marriage nonsense, so there's no risk there.

Why not?

His rumbling words come hot as fire as they lash against my cheek. "I won't be gentle."

"I don't want you to be." And if he doesn't believe my words, he must believe my body, my breaths coming quicker, my nipples straining against the dress. My sex wetter around his fingers. My hand is cupping his and I press my fingers against his. "More."

"Greedy girl." A dark chuckle vibrates through him. His fingers dip deeper, his whole hand hugging my sex as he presses his thumb against my clit like it's a button, turning on the orgasm, the building tension in my body becoming shudders. Burst after burst of release rushes through me, my fingers clutching at his.

"Oh God..."

His fingers leave me, going to my waist. He's pushing my panties down over my hips. He gets them to my knees and they fall away. I step out of them, suddenly fearful of the unknown. My knees feel weak, and I lean against the wall for support.

Is this really happening?

Then his mouth is back on mine, telling me it is. His kiss is hungry and demanding, his tongue swiping against mine as his hands go under my dress, clutching at my bare ass. He growls into our kiss. "Mine."

He brings one hand to my hair, tugging at the back of my neck as he kisses me.

My hands go to his belt, my fingers trembling. I've never done this before. I feign confidence I don't feel as I unbuckle his belt. He moans into our kiss when he feels my fingers brush his growing cock as I undo the button of his pants, lowering his zipper.

He captures my wrist, lifts my arm, and pins my hand to the wall above my head. He grabs my other hand, his fingers smoothing up my bare arm as he lifts it to meet the other.

I'm powerless, panty-less, pinned to the wall, hands useless, imprisoned above my outstretched arms.

I've never felt freer in my life.

He circles both wrists with just his forefinger and thumb, keeping my hands trapped. The fingertips of his other hand slowly drag over my skin, fingers lightly raking my skin, sending chills over my entire body.

He grabs my sex over my dress. "This belongs to me."

And his mouth is back on mine, hot and greedy. He rucks up my dress, bringing the material high around my waist. The cool night air dances up my bare legs.

I feel the head of his cock between my thighs. I'm surprised by the softness of the skin that surrounds the hardness of his manhood. Soft but hard, pressing against me with need.

My mind goes blank, unsure and overwhelmed, but my pussy comes even more awake at his nearness, arousal flooding between my thighs. My body knows what to do, my legs parting. I lift my knee, dragging it up the side of his body, hooking my calf around his waist.

Thank God for Charlie's vibrator. I think I'm less anxious, knowing I've at least had something inside me already.

He gives a growl, grabbing my ass harder, pulling me into him. He has to let my arms go to grab his cock and I'm grateful because all I want to do is run my hands through his hair, hug his neck and feel close to him.

He centers the head at the entrance of my sex. I go up on the ball of my foot, stretching, but it's not enough, he's so tall. He abandons his attempt, instead grabbing me under my ass, lifting me around him till both legs are wrapped around his muscular torso, my ankles locked behind his lower back.

My skin brushes against the wall as he moves. Now, he's got one hand beneath me holding me up against him. The other goes to his cock and he lines the head up with my entrance.

"Look at me, little pet. I want your eyes on mine."

"Don't call me that and I will," I say, locking my arms around his neck.

His dark eyes flash with anger, hating to be disobeyed, but I hold firm and what he sees in my gaze makes him relent. He teases my wet, wanting entrance, rubbing the silky head of his cock against me.

I let out a moan, my insides clenching, desperate to feel what it's like to have a man inside of me. Will it be like the vibrator Charlie left me, or better?

"What shall I call you then?" He leans in, giving a lick and a nip at my collarbone.

"I don't know." I can barely breathe. It will be better than the vibrator...

He nips at my earlobe. "How about 'my sweet babygirl?'"

My sex answers the question, pulsing with arousal. "I like that."

"Then come here, my sweet babygirl, and give yourself to me."

He pushes inside me. My sex is tight, stretching to let him in. There's pain. He's so big and I'm small, but as he moves further inside me, the pain turns into a warm, liquid pleasure.

His hand wraps around the back of my neck. "Mine. All mine, babygirl. And I'm not going to be gentle."

With that, he thrusts his hips up, hard, impaling me with the full length of his cock. I can feel it all the way up in my throat where my heart gets stuck, my breath a choked gasp as he tears into me with his size.

Before I can recover enough to make a sound, his mouth is back on mine, his tongue pushing hard against mine. I can't think. Can't breathe. I'm nothing but the feel of his mouth on mine, his fingers digging into my neck...

And his massive member pulling back out of me. I'm a virgin in every sense of the word, but I lost my hymen horseback riding years ago, and the session with the vibrator prepared me slightly for this but still, I'm overwhelmed in every sense of the word.

Nothing could have prepared me for having him inside me, his chest pressed against me, pinning me to the wall, my legs wrapped around his waist, his hands in my hair. He thrusts up again, fucking me with his entire cock all at once.

Emotions swirl through me as I realize what I've done. I've betrayed my family by giving myself to this man... I want him, I want this and...

"I can't take it..."

"You can take it, babygirl. You can take all of me." He pulls back, the head of his cock teasing my entrance and now, instead of thinking I can't take it, I feel helplessly empty. I want to beg for it.

"Please..."

"I like it when you beg, sweet girl. You sound so pretty." He gives a laugh, his teeth nipping at the sensitive skin at the base of my neck. But he gives me what I want, propelling forward, his cock diving into me again.

I don't know if it's a moan or a whine, but the sound is more animal than human as it rises from my throat. "Oh, God... it hurts but it feels good."

"You said to ruin you."

His words make my sex clench around him, holding him to me, making him *mine.*

My body freezes, the hairs on the back of my neck standing on end.

The sound of the pin in the door lock.

My heart lurches into my throat.

Liam's body tenses, ready to kill. "Who is that?"

"I don't know." I shake my head, waiting for a face to appear in the doorway.

Liam slips from me and my feet go to the floor. He pulls my dress down to cover my legs, his cock very much present, standing at attention.

The very surprised face of my brother Mattia slides in between the door and the doorframe. His gaze goes from my flushed face and wrinkled dress to the third person in the room, Liam's massive cock.

"Uh?"

I breathe, "Mattia!"

"Oh, shit. I thought you were alone." Mattia takes in Liam and me, realizing what's happening. "You aren't going to marry John, are you?"

I shake my head.

"Good. I haven't been a perfect brother, I know that, but I couldn't stand the thought of you with that old man. I've been trying to think of a way to stop it myself." Mattia glances over his shoulder, toward the stairs. "You can't be here in the morning. Go now. I'll cover for you."

I look to Liam. He gives me a nod, stuffing his cock back in his pants, straightening his clothing and buckling his belt.

"Come. Now." Liam holds his hand out to me, his dark eyes glittering at me.

If I take his hand, I'm going against my family, leaving them without the fortune they crave. I'm heading out into the dark night with a man I don't know whether I should trust. If I go with him now, I must accept that no matter what turbulence dances between us, we are in this together.

I place my hand in his. "Let's go."

LIAM

SHE LOOKS SO BEAUTIFUL, SITTING BESIDE ME ON MY JET. LIKE SHE belongs here. Young and fresh, her cheeks still flushed from our hurried exit.

She wears soft, light-colored jeans and a cropped sweater, tossed on after a quick shower back at my place while my staff quickly packed our things. She stares out the window at the dark night sky, a happy smile set on her rosy lips. "I've never left Italy," she says. "I can't believe it. Do I need a passport?"

"No." We'll be flying straight to the island, landing on the stretch of tarmac that runs along the northern side of the island. "There is no customs at the Parish."

Her nose crinkles adorably. "Why do they call the island the Parish?"

"The man that founded it for the family started with nothing but a few boats he bought off a priest."

"My first time leaving the country and I'm going to a private island..."

"There's a first time for everything." I slip my fingers up the inside of her denim-covered thighs, thinking of the feeling of entering her for the first time.

"Well, half a first time," she says. She looks up at me from under her lashes. "We have to finish what we started."

"Soon," I promise.

She leans her head back against the headrest, a little laugh bubbling up. "Did you see my brother's face? God. That was priceless."

"Priceless, yes." But there will be a price.

Her brother witnessed the catalyst for the beginning of a war. I haven't taken her without consequences. In a matter of a few hours, the sun will rise, and John Romano will find himself standing alone at the altar.

A humiliated Accardi at his side.

Lance Romano allows us to ship our weapons to his seaside estate. They're then transported along the river to the old Russo castle for storage, where Luca and Esme Romano now rule. Without the Romanos on our side, we lose access to valuable land along the sea. Trade routes.

There will be revenge from both sides, directed at me. I need to tell Rockland, the head of the Bachman family, what's happened. To prepare him. He's already at the Parish, our private island off the coast of Greece. He'll meet with us tomorrow.

He'll support my decision to take the girl. But I'm afraid of what he's going to ask from me in return. I don't know that I can agree to his demands.

I slip my hand from her thigh.

Staff dressed in sleek black suits bring us flutes of champagne. I take hers away with a shake of my head before she can have a sip. I get a pout in return.

Does she have to be this enchanting?

She dives into the snacks they brought, cheese and bread and fruit. Her lips are stained with the juice of red strawberries from the bowl of berries. "These are so flavorful. How did you get them this time of year?"

"We have them flown in from Florida."

"And the bread?" She takes a delicate nibble of the crispy crust.

"Baked fresh daily. Brought in from Rome."

She smears a bit of blueberry goat cheese onto the bread, popping it in her mouth. "Mmm..." Her eyes roll to the back of her head as she chews.

"What have you been eating at home?"

She takes a sip of sparkling water, dabbing at her mouth with her cloth napkin. "Not much. I'm afraid I'm not a very good cook. I'm also not allowed to go to the shops alone, so we eat a lot of sandwiches. But with processed cheese and meats on that crappy thin white bread. Nothing like this."

"If you're impressed by this small snack, you're going to lose your mind when they serve you a five-course meal at the Parish."

Her eyes drag up to mine. "Really?"

I nod. "The head of the family, Rockland, and his wife, Tess, are coming to Greece. Whenever that happens, the family goes all out. There will be drinks and dancing, followed by a sit-down dinner, then more partying."

"Wow. I can't wait." Her brow furrows a beat, and she looks back at me. "Why are they coming to the Parish?"

"To meet you."

Her mouth drops open, the bread forgotten in her hand. The color leaves her cheeks.

"Me?"

"Yes," I say. "You."

12

E *milia*

A FEW BUTTONS OF HIS CRISP, BLUE SHIRT ARE UNDONE, REVEALING part of a circular tattoo covering the upper left half of his chest. I glance at the markings. "Does that mean anything special?"

He nods. "Brotherhood." He leaves it at that.

As hot as the peek of his tattoo and tan chest is, the view of the Parish from the jet window steals my attention. Perfectly manicured lawns of bright green grass surround white stone mansions, decorative wrought iron railings wrap around balconies that seem to float in the cloudless blue sky. All white buildings except for one that's been painted... pink.

The largest of these meticulously maintained mansions is the one the women in this family have claimed for their own.

They call it the "B-Hive," named after the dozens of Beauties buzzing inside of its walls.

I call it heaven.

As soon as we land, the women whisk me into their pink paradise. There's not a man in sight.

The staff is comprised of older females, those who have put in their time and can no longer stand on their feet all day. They sit on the veranda, drinking wine and laughing. The Beauties serve the women, refilling their glasses and bringing them charcuterie trays they've had younger staff members leave at a table by the back door of the Hive.

I'm lying on a grape-colored crushed velvet chaise by a corner window where I have a view of the blue-green sea, its waves crashing to the white sand beach in foamy bursts. I'm sipping freshly squeezed orange juice laced with pomegranate, a fluffy white robe tucked around my waxed, polished, and moisturized skin that's just been pampered at their in-house spa.

Beauties surround me, lounging around in their own robes, chatting idly with one another, sipping champagne.

They're all very relaxed... with a few exceptions.

There's a small group of women taking me in with serious gazes. I guess I'm what they'd call a tomboy. Up to that one perfect morning getting ready in the bathroom in my suite at Liam's, my self-care routine consisted of scrubbing my hair with off-brand shampoo before I ran out of lukewarm water and sometimes painting my nails red with polish from the drugstore.

Charlie directs a head-to-toe makeover attempt. A woman named Sasha stands at Charlie's side, her long, dark, business-like ponytail flowing down her back.

Sasha says, "Raw beauty. A diamond in the rough, for sure. But after a lifetime trapped with men?" She lifts my hand in hers. "Just look at these cuticles. We need the mani-pedi team here, stat."

Sasha shakes her head while I glance down at my hand, wondering what a cuticle is and what makes mine so bad.

"Sorry?" I ask.

"It's okay. Not your fault," Sasha says, accepting my apology.

She's taking this so seriously it makes me laugh. I bring my glass to my lips to hide the giggle, taking a sip of my juice. It's bright and tangy and icy cold.

Charlie speaks to me in a soothing voice, like she's approaching a wounded animal. "About your hair."

My hand flutters to my hair, tangled from where Liam had pinned me up against my bedroom wall last night. Do I make excuses for the nest? "Sorry, ladies, it got a little tangled when I was..."

Losing my virginity?

"When you were on the plane. Yes, of course. That happens." Charlie fingers one of my long, tangled locks. "How would you feel about taking off a few inches. Maybe some highlights?"

"Hair dye? No, thank you. But I'd love to lose some of this hair. It's..." Do I tell them how the men of my family control me, trying to mold me into whatever shape they think the highest bidding man would want? How they won't let me cut my hair? I finish with, "A burden."

Charlie smiles. "I think it's beautiful natural. If we have them take off a few inches, it'll take care of the split ends and give you a fresh look."

"Thanks. Sorry I'm in such bad shape. I've never done this stuff before."

"We've seen worse." Sasha nods toward a woman with a friendly face and dirty blonde hair named Hannah.

Hannah pushes past Sasha, giving her an accusatory look. "What Sasha was *trying* to say is that you are drop-dead gorgeous and we're just here to polish you up. It's so much fun. Trust me."

"What?" Sasha lifts her hands, shrugging to show her innocence. "I called her a *diamond.*"

I defuse the disagreement. "Well, I was in the rough. I have a lot of brothers."

Hannah nods. "We need our space from guys sometimes. It's nice to have a place for just *us.*"

They are including me in their *us,* and it feels. So. Good.

Two women come rushing in from the spa, tugging silver suitcases on wheels behind them. In a blink, they've got an entire nail salon set up around me, something I've seen in movies but never gotten a chance to experience in real life, of course.

They soak my fingers and toes in warm, lavender-scented water.

As they pamper me, I take in the women in the room. They're all so achingly beautiful, but that's not what makes me happy to be here with them. It's the smiles on their faces. The way their arms lean against one another's, so comfortable with each other, or even the way one woman's head rests on another's shoulder as they laugh over photos on her phone screen.

I've never had that.

With any woman other than my mother. And she died when I was ten.

Is it possible that women *need* good female companionship to be well-adjusted?

I can't wait to spend the next undefined amount of time finding out.

"All done," the manicurist says with a smile.

I look down at my perfectly painted white shellac nails. "Thank you so much."

Oh God. Do I pay her, do I tip?

I whisper to Sasha, "I have no money."

Her brow furrows. "Sweetheart. Didn't anyone tell you? This is an all-expenses-paid kind of place. Just enjoy. You don't have to think about, pay for, or do a thing. Liam was very clear; anything you want, everything you want, and only the best for you."

"Oh... he... ordered this?" I settle back in my chaise, admiring how my fingers look holding the stem of my fancy glass.

"Of course he did." She rolls her eyes. "The man is obviously obsessed with you."

He's obsessed with you.

Her words stick with me. I go to deny them, but then I think of how he's always coming into my life, chasing me down with no encouragement from me, and the denial dries up on my tongue. I sip my juice.

Hmm... maybe he is a little obsessed. I look around at all the privileges I'm experiencing. Is a little obsession so bad?

Sasha whips out her phone, ready to take notes. "So, what are Liam's preferences? Likes? Dislikes? Favorite color? Preferred neckline, dress length?"

I laugh, picturing Liam in a dress. "Wait. Are we putting me in a gown? Or him?"

Sasha smirks. "You, but don't you want him to love it?"

I think about it a moment. I appreciate what he's done for me but I'm tired of pleasing men. "I'd like to look the way that I would like to look. If that's okay."

Sasha sinks down onto the chaise beside me. "But we are trying to get him to propose, right? That's the purpose of this whole makeover mission? To put the icing on the cake and have him give in to his already obvious attraction to you and—"

"No." I shake my head. That was *so not* the plan. "I don't want to get married."

There's a collective gasp from the women.

Charlie's pink fingertips flutter to her chest. "Ever?"

The horror on her face makes me giggle.

"No," I say. "I mean, when you've dealt with demanding men all your life, you really don't want to tie yourself to one for all of eternity."

Sasha goes into bossy mode, acting in a way I imagine an older sister might. She throws an arm over my shoulders. "Being married to a man is different than being related to one. Especially a Bachman man. Let me tell you some of the highlights of my marriage. Starting with last night. Oh. My. God. There's this vibrating pair of panties that Carter just—"

"Sasha. Stop." Hannah puts a hand over Sasha's to gently shut her up. Hannah pastes a bright smile on her face. "Emilia is totally right. We need to do this makeover for her. Not for any man. Now, ask Emilia her preferences."

I think of my spandex leggings and bike shorts. My cropped tees and sweatshirts. My sneakers. My ponytail. With no mom, no sisters, no shopping, and a limited budget, it hits me. "I... honestly don't know what I like when it comes to that stuff."

"Well, we *cannot* have that." A woman in a short white dress and red high heels pushes her way through the crowd. She's all business with her red hair pulled high in a bun, thick red plastic frames on the tip of her cute, ski-slope nose.

I have no idea who this woman is, but I like her already.

I hold my hand out. "Hi, I'm Emilia."

She takes it, shaking it daintily. "Emilia, lovely to meet you. I'm Jules and luckily—I'm here to save the day. If you don't know what you like, I'll help you find it." She pushes the glasses up the bridge of her nose, whispering, "These are fake by the way, they just make me feel legit."

"I like them!" I laugh.

Jules pats her hand against the massive book she holds in her hands.

"Thank you. Like I said, I'm Jules, and this"—she holds the book up with reverence— "is the Beauty Bible."

All the women giggle, filling the room with dramatic oohs and aahs.

I stare down at the glossy white cover of the hardbacked book. It's massive, filling her whole lap. The cover is swooshes of gold gilt, the words *Beauties' Bible* scrolled out across the front in sparkling letters. "Did you make this?"

"Guilty!" she purrs. "When I joined the family, I took on events at the castle—"

I swallow. Hard. "You guys have your own castle?"

"Of course! I love throwing weddings there." She gives my ribs a nudge with her elbow. "Keep that in mind just in case."

I laugh. "Okay."

"When I took over as the event planner there, I started making these 'look books' to display the choices the bride and groom had for candle displays, flower arrangements, decorations for the main hall, all the things. I guess I got a little carried away with my organization and—"

"Jules is *very* organized," a younger woman with dark hair pitches in. "I'm Ella, by the way."

I smile. "Nice to meet you."

"Thank you, Ella." Jules gives me a smile. "Ella's my number one fan because her wedding was my first. You never forget your first. Anyway, knee-deep in event prep organizing, I got to thinking that whenever a new woman joins us, it must be a bit overwhelming choosing so many beautiful things all at once. Most of us come from simple backgrounds and didn't know designers or anything about fashion."

"But Jules did. She had her own fashion blog in the city," Ella says.

"Back when a blog was a thing, but yes, I had a basic knowledge of where to start, but not everyone does. There's so much to learn. To choose from." Jules flips the book open. "First things first. We have to do your colors."

"My colors?" I parrot back. What does that mean?

I hope my colors aren't as bad as my cuticles.

She nods. "Based on your hair color, eye color, and skin tone, we find your season. Then we can match makeup shades to you as well as narrow down which color clothing looks best on you."

My clothes are black and white. Sometimes gray. Period. "People... do that?" I ask.

She nods. "Yes. And trust me. Once you've started wearing clothing that complements your skin tone, you'll never go back."

She flips through the pages, slipping colorful papers from pockets, holding them up to my face. She has a thin crinkly sheet of gold and one of silver and she puts those against the tops of my arms, making notes.

It's a very serious process. Her face is stoic, the other Beauties looking over her shoulder, practically holding their breath as she works.

"It's trickier than it seems," Ella whispers in my ear. "Not everyone can do it."

Sasha nods. "Jules is the master."

Jules carefully turns my arm over, her fingertips running up the faint veins that show there. "Mmm... hmm. Just as I suspected. Green."

"Green?" I look down at my arm. My veins *are* a green color. "I thought all veins were blue."

Too busy making notes to answer, finally she raises her head, bright eyes meeting mine. "It's as I suspected, but of course, one has to trust the process." She stands, looking around the room. "We have a Clear Spring joining us, ladies! Just in time for the Springtime Ball tomorrow night."

Charlie claps her hands. "Ooh, and the pre-dinner and dance tonight."

"You all have a dance to celebrate your dance?" I ask.

Sasha furrows her brows at me. "Of course, we do! And the day after the Ball?"

"We throw a brunch!" Hannah says. "If you didn't know by our curves, Beauties love to eat. I freaking love the food here. Wait till you have one of the freshly baked croissants. To *die* for!" She rolls her eyes, collapsing on a bed. "I had two this morning."

Jules says, "The Bachmans make up any excuse to party and who doesn't love spring? It deserves multiple celebrations."

"I'm a Spring." I think of the roses in my mother's garden. "My favorite season."

Jules sits back down, quickly filling me in on all the rules I must follow as a Spring or face the uncertain future of looking... *dun... dun... dun...* washed out. The girls give a collective gasp at that.

Her fingertips stroke the paper, running over tiny squares of colors that form one large square filling the page. She stops on a unique shade of taupe-y purple that I've never owned in my life.

I say, "It reminds me of wisteria."

"Dewberry," Jules says. "That shall be your signature color."

"Amen." Sasha gives a solemn nod. "I wore nothing but black before meeting Jules, but she has changed me forever and now I will die on a Pistachio Green hill."

Ella raises a pale hand. "Sapphire Blue."

Hannah points to her light gray cardigan. "Baby Dove Gray."

Jules points a toe of her high heel. "Fire Engine Red, of course."

I stare at the pretty color. "It's lovely. Can we change the name though?" I don't know why but Dewberry just sounds off to me.

"Sure," Jules laughs. "How about..."

Charlie puts a hand on my shoulder. "How about Emeria. For Emilia and wisteria."

"Emeria," I say. "I love it."

Jules shoots a few texts from her phone. "I'll get some samples in different fabrics up here ASAP. We need to see what you like against your skin. What type of material do you normally wear?"

"Uh... spandex?"

Sasha looks me over, the tip of her tongue running along her lips. "I'm getting a vibe off you. You're so... sensual. I think you're going to be a silk and satin girl."

The confession falls from my pomegranate-flavored tongue. "I was a never-been-kissed virgin until a few hours ago." My cheeks flush.

Did I say that out loud?

The room goes dead quiet. I expected laughter, or at least, polite giggling. Instead, a chill runs through the air.

I glance around the room, a ball of ice forming in my belly. "What did I say?"

Finally, the room thaws. The silence is gone. Their comments come at me like lightning bolts in a storm, striking one after the other.

"Let me get this straight," Jules says. "You're the daughter—"

Sasha interjects, crossing her arms over her chest. "Only daughter."

Jules speaks slowly, keeping her eyes on me. "Only daughter of the head of a mafia family—"

Sasha nods. "In Northern Italy, the most wild and rugged of the Italian mafia turfs—"

Jules says, "And Liam took your..."

"V-card?" I offer.

Hannah puts a hand to her forehead, shaking her head. "Oh. Shit."

Ella's pale face has gone alabaster. She tries to smile, but it looks more like a terrified grin. She takes my hand in hers. "I know you think you don't want to get married, but really, it's lovely."

"You're going to love being married," Jules nods empathically.

Ella keeps smiling at me. "We can help you, you know, adjust to married life."

"And you'll officially be one of us," Jules offers.

Hannah speaks with a false lilt in her tone. "Imagine. No more brothers but all these sisters as besties to look after you!"

"And you'll be a billionaire," Sasha says. "Seriously. Liam will give you a black Amex."

I shake my head, overwhelmed by their ping-ponging comments. "I don't understand. I told you, I'm not getting married."

But they keep going, fake brightness in their voices, to convince me this whole marriage thing is a great idea. I can't even keep the voices straight, unsure who each one belongs to as they speak.

"And we can take you shopping."

"And do lunches."

"And Liam's so hot and protective. Seriously, he has a hard exterior, I know, but Liam is a cinnamon roll on the inside."

"Like when you burn a marshmallow, and the outside is black and charred but the inside is gooey—"

"Oh, yes. So gooey. Those are the best kind, don't you think?"

"What are you all saying?" I ask.

All eyes turn to me as they practically speak in unison. "Rockland."

I think back to what Liam said on the jet. "Rockland? Liam said he's the head of the family and we're meeting with him tomorrow. What about him?"

"And Tess, his wife." Jules adds. "Gotta throw in my fellow ginger. She's just as much the boss as he is, in my eyes. And they are going to demand he marry you."

"What?" Equal parts ice and heat creep through my veins, thinking of Liam.

Charlie takes the reins, her tone firm but kind. "Look, Emilia. If Liam took your virginity and you were promised to another family, you all kind of don't have any choice except to marry. It's the best way to try to smooth things over. You know. Liam could beg forgiveness from your father and the injured party and say he was just so head-over-heels in love he couldn't not have you for himself. Then, he could fulfill the contract to your father, maybe throw in a little extra for the inconvenience."

Ella nods emphatically. "Everyone understands the desperation of young love."

"It could work." Jules nods.

"It *has* to work," Hannah says. "You have no other choice."

"Oh, they have a choice, alright," Sasha snaps.

All eyes focus on me.

Sasha tosses her ponytail over her shoulder like a weapon. The look she gives me makes a chill run down my spine. "They could *not* marry. And start a war. Putting every single one of us in danger."

My stomach twists, the idea of the upcoming meeting with Rockland and Tess filling me with doom. I don't want to marry. The idea of being spiritually and legally bound to a man? It terrifies me.

But I can't start a war, especially not now that I see the faces of those who would be fighting for me.

What have we done?

13

L *iam*

THE DREAM IS THE SAME EVERY TIME. THE ROOM FILLS WITH A SMOKE-
like cloud, her pulling away, disappearing further into the haze. I
chase her down, but she's always just out of my reach, my fingers
grasping at tendrils of dissipating smoke. I shout till my voice goes
hoarse, my throat raw. The words never change.

No. Don't leave me, Emily. Please.

I wake, my heart heavy from the dream, my head aching from the
travel and time difference.

I shower and dress, in no mood for the ball tonight. Our
impromptu visit lined up with one of the monthly celebrations the
family loves to throw. This month we have a dinner and dance
tonight, to celebrate tomorrow night's Springtime Ball, an evening
dedicated to celebrating nothing more complicated than the warm
weather and budding greens and flowers of the season.

The ball is also the kick-off to the Beauty's charity season. They may dress up and show off the latest fashions, parading around in their couture gowns, but the women are beyond generous and they host public events each year to bring awareness and raise money for the many charities they support.

I join the men at the bar. The brothers are giving one another shit, laughing as they sip their imported whiskey. I stand off to the side, holding down the far end of the bar, in no mood for banter. I tip my glass back, sending all the liquor sliding down my throat in one pass.

I feel cold. The liquor helps, warming me from the inside. I put my empty glass on the marble bar top for a refill.

Where is she?

The moment the jet landed, like a swarm of bees, the Beauties surrounded her, carrying her off. Emilia didn't even give one glance over her shoulder as they pulled her away. It was like she was relieved to be out of my presence.

I knock back the second drink. I need to relax. Tonight is for pleasure. Tomorrow, Rockland and Tess will be here and then... well...

Conversations need to be had.

I push the whole thinking-of-the-consequences-of-my-rash-actions cloud away.

Not tonight.

Women start to trickle into the room, each one dressed in a color to complement their skin tone, cut to highlight the most alluring parts of their unique figures. Where is my girl?

My sweet babygirl...

I shake my head. What's gotten into me? Bury my cock inside her one time and now I'm thinking of her as *my* girl?

Po takes my silence and the fact that I don't have him pinned to the wall by his throat right now as a good sign.

He keeps going. "Look. That was terrible, the whole thing you went through with Emily—"

My dark eyes turn on him. He knows not to say her name.

He clears his throat, doubling down. "What you went through as Liam Black was hell, but now, you're Liam Bachman. And maybe it's time to move on. Maybe it's time to do the stuff."

I twist the now half-full glass, watching the liquor slosh around the sides, repeating his words. "Do the stuff."

"Yeah. Like relationships. And marriage. And... what the hell." He flashes a smile so rich I almost smile back. "Maybe even love."

Love.

The four-letter word makes my insides grow cold again. My throat feels tight. I sip at my drink, my head loose from the first two whiskeys I downed.

I can't go back there. Even if Po thinks it's possible, I know better. It's not.

Our conversation hits a natural lull. He drinks and I smoke as we quietly contemplate the world together but separate. We watch as a woman carrying a cut crystal vase of flowers passes us.

She trips.

The vase falls from her hands, barreling toward the stone floor, bursting into a million shards of glass as it hits. Water explodes around her feet, the flowers laid out on the floor.

A warning.

Po, always the gentleman, goes to help her. She smiles up at him. Her savior. She'll be in his bed by the end of the night. Other staff come to help clean it up. They don't glue the pieces of the vase back together, do they? No. They don't even try. Instead, they sweep up the mess with brooms and bins, making sure not to leave any bit of glass behind.

When something shatters, it can't be put back together.

I bend down, lifting one single rose from the wreckage. The color reminds me of the blush in Emilia's cheeks. I inhale the soft scent. When I stand...

There she is...

Emilia hovers at the entrance to the ballroom, all nerves and beauty. She's stunning. A million times more beautiful than the flower I hold in my hand. How could I compare the color of its petals to her skin?

She's radiance.

My breath catches as I take her in. Her face is carefully made up, light makeup to accentuate her full lips, thick lashes, high cheek-bones. Her hair hangs to her shoulders, smooth and sleek. She wears a lilac gown, her skin radiant against the shade of purple.

Her hands are clutched together like she's nervous. Her tight gaze scans the room, reminding me of a kid at her first middle school dance.

Wait—*is* this her first dance?

"Emilia." I move toward her.

Her eyes find mine. "Liam."

I feel... strange. The desire to be a gentleman, to make her feel every bit as enchanting as she is, to make her smile, to be... kind.

I hand her the rose. "For you."

"Thank you." She dips her nose into the soft petals. "A David Austin rose. My mother grew these."

I put a hand on her waist, gathering the silk under my fingers, the heat of her skin radiating through the thin fabric of the gown. "You look so beautiful."

The hand with the rose lazily slips around my shoulders. Her hip presses against my thigh. She nods at my black tux, fingering the ends of my slicked-back hair. "You look even more handsome than usual. Didn't think that was possible."

Are we... *flirting?*

Flirting is just another thing listed under the overarching umbrella of stuff I don't do. So why am I leaning in, inhaling her scent, and whispering into her ear, "It's only possible because my face changes when I see you. I go from an ogre to something... lighter."

She laughs, giving my shoulder a playful swat with her fingers. "You could never be an ogre."

"Are you sure?" I kiss her earlobe, my lips trailing along the curve of her ear. "I believe I've been called a monster more than once."

She hesitates in my arms. "I did think you were a monster at one time." But then she melts against me, her cheek brushing against mine. "But I don't anymore."

We sway together, our bodies made for this dance, made for one another. We fit perfectly together.

The beauty with her beast.

"What changed?" I ask, my fingers stroking lines along her lower back. Salt air from a breeze off the Adriatic floats through the glass doors that have been fully opened, taking away one wall so it's like we're dancing by the ocean.

"I don't know," she says. "I think you've just been giving me these glimpses of yourself." Her eyes catch mine as she clarifies her statement with, "Your *real* self. The one you hide from everyone else."

My chest feels tight. I focus on keeping my voice low and steady. "Is that so?" She does this to me, makes me think before I speak, makes me work to keep her from cracking my stony exterior, the hard shell that was an extension of myself until she came into my life.

"Yes. Like small things. Apologizing to me in my room. Handing me this rose." She brings it to my cheek, dragging the soft, silky petals across my freshly shaven skin.

"It was nothing. A woman dropped a vase and—"

"And big things too." Her gray-green eyes focus on mine, a captivating smile curling on her pouty lips. She stops swaying, standing still in my arms. "Like risking it all to bring me here."

The truth hangs between us like a thread of spider's silk. One disturbance and it'll be broken, snapped in two, the pieces sailing away from one another. What can I do? Lie? Deny? Tell her it will all be alright. That there is a way out of this web without binding the two of us for eternity...

I don't feel like lying anymore.

"Come here, Emilia." I hold her close. "Come here and dance with me."

She goes to speak but I take her words with a gentle kiss.

And we dance.

14

E *milia*

AT DINNER I'M SO KEYED UP, EVEN JUST HIS ARM BRUSHING MINE AS he cuts his filet makes shivers run through my body. He takes my hand afterward, leading me to my room. The electricity between us is undeniable. Anticipation settles heavy in my core.

I can't wait to rekindle what we did last night, to explore his body and this time, to take my time and...

"I have to go." He brushes a chaste kiss on my cheek. He opens the door, waiting for me to go inside. Alone.

Rejection, queasy and cool, creeps into my belly. "You're not staying with me?"

"No. I can't." He shakes his head. "You gave me what I wanted. I gave you what you wanted. Things are already... *complicated...*

between us. Let's not tangle ourselves further till we speak to Rockland."

He doesn't want to tangle with me. And all I want to do is wrap myself up in him.

Do not cry, Emilia.

One rose, one dance, does not earn your tears.

"Okay!" I say, too brightly. "See you in the morning."

But when morning comes, a little devil is on my shoulder, whispering in my ear, telling me that if he won't have me, I can at least make it as difficult as possible for him.

Determination fills me as I tear through the drawers where my things have been unpacked. I toss aside the leggings, the jeans, finally finding the drawers filled with underthings the staff carefully folded for me.

Bathing suits. Yes!

I pull the first one from the drawer. A red one-piece, a bow tied between the breasts. Cute but too modestly cut for my purposes.

I think back to the Beauties I had the most interaction with yesterday. One sticks out in my mind as the woman who would have what I need. She's a Winter, but we can make this work.

I call a staff member by pressing the top of a fake brass bell that sits on the nightstand, who calls Sasha for me on the intercom. "Sasha," I say. "I need to borrow something."

I have them let Liam know I'll be meeting him on the beach today. No need to come pick me up.

Sasha brings me what I need, waiting impatiently in the bedroom while I change in the bath. When I come out, her eyes go wide.

"Holy shit!" she says. "Va va va voom! He's going to lose his mind."

"Can you help me with the straps?" I ask, unsure if I've got this booby trap on correctly.

She gets it tied just right, then helps me with my hair, curling it around my face. She does my makeup, bronzer and pink cheeks and gold shadow.

"Natural and sun-kissed," she says, looking over her work.

When she's done, I look in the mirror, hardly able to believe it's me looking back.

It turns out there's a deep shade of blue that looks great on either a Winter or a Spring. Especially when you're only wearing a scrap of it.

I spot him on the shore, his tan, toned body stretched out on a white lounger. My heart literally skips a beat, jumping and bouncing against my ribs at the sight of his half-naked body.

The man is hot with a capital HOT.

Beautiful people wander the beach. Many of the men have tattoos on their chests like his, an intricate black circular design with leaf-like spokes coming from its center, each one uniquely decorated within its thick border.

I strut out onto the beach, fully confident that I look amazing, that I was made for this moment, and when he sees me, he's going to growl with total and absolute agony from unfulfilled desire and take me into his arms and rush me right up to my bedroom and—

Nope. He's pissed.

"What." He rises from his lounger, hands going to his trim waist. "The hell. Is that."

Hmm... I got the growl, but not the reaction I was expecting. I move as gracefully as possible, rolling my hips under the thin side straps of the bikini.

"You don't like it?" I shimmy over to the open chair beside him. I throw open my oversized designer bag—forgot the name of the designer but know it cost a fortune—and dig around for the all-natural, organic, anti-aging sunscreen Jules forced upon me. I find the tube, handing it to him.

"Could you do my back? This top is so tiny, I'm afraid I'll get burned."

He doesn't take the sunscreen, choosing to pace the sand in front of me instead.

"I specifically said one-piece. Where are the swimsuits I told them to order for you?" He gestures wildly at the masterpiece of strings and tiny silky triangles showcasing my curves.

"The suits you bought are safe and sound in the drawers in my room," I say.

"Why aren't you wearing one of them?" There's that growl again.

I do a little twirl, showing off my barely covered ass. "You don't like?"

"I like. I love. And so will every other man out here with a pulse. Do you know how many single brothers are here for the Ball, just cruising around looking for a single girl?"

"There are no single girls here." I correct myself. "Well, aside from me."

He narrows his eyes at me. "Exactly."

I wanted to make him want me. Judging by the suspicious bulge in the front of his swim trunks, mission accomplished. But something else is going on here.

I eye him. "Wait. Are you... jealous?"

"Jealous?" He rubs his hand over the back of his neck. "What do I have to be jealous of? Every man here saw me dance with you last night. They all know if they so much as speak to you, I'll rip their tongues out."

"That's a bit over-the-top, isn't it?" I say.

"What's over-the-top is that suit you're wearing and how much of your body you're showing off to the men here." He points up to the mansion. "Go change. Now."

"No."

He comes closer, his voice rumbling in my ear. "Go change or so help me God, I will tear this suit off you right here, right now, and take you."

A delicious thrill runs through me. I smooth my fingers over his cheek. "Don't tempt me."

He gives a furious growl.

I move in close, slipping a hand along his stubbled jaw. I whisper in his ear, "I wore this for you."

He freezes, his face pressed against my hand. "You wanted to tempt me, didn't you? Because of last night. Because I wouldn't go to bed with you."

His words sting but I plow through them, playing my game. "You made a mistake, leaving me all alone." I tug on the ends of my suit strings. "This is your punishment."

Now his hand slides up my face. "You're not the one who doles out punishments, little girl."

I want to snap back with an angry retort, but my mind turns to sand, my mouth sawdust.

He grabs my ass in his hands, clutching at my curves. "Last chance. Change or I spank you. Right here. Right now. On this beach."

"You wouldn't dare. And besides, I thought you threatened to take me, not to spank me—hey! What are you doing?" His hand comes down right across the center of my ass. If the sound of his palm hitting my skin doesn't get the attention of everyone on the beach, my string of expletives does.

"Ooh shit! That hurts. What the hell, Liam!"

"Watch your mouth when you're with me." He drags me over to the lounger, taking a seat and pinning me to his lap. He slaps my ass again, my curves jiggling upon impact. He tightens his arm around my waist.

"So now I can't cuss either? You're going to dictate my wardrobe and my language? I don't think so—" The feel of his fingers tugging at the waistband of my suit stops my original sentence. "Wait... what are you doing?"

I throw a look over my shoulder to confirm the man is not doing what I think he is.

He is.

His fingers are tucking under the straps of my bathing suit bottoms, inching the spandex down over my curves. I feel the top of my crack exposed to the warm sun. The bottoms weren't much, but they were something, and now horror and dread fill me as I realize everyone on this beach is about to see my bare ass.

"Liam Bachman. Don't you dare!"

"Or what, little girl? What are you going to do?" He gives a dark chuckle, pulling my suit down, settling it around the tops of my thighs.

He turns his body so I'm laid out over his lap, a line along the horizon, his body between me and the people on the beach. His big chest and back shelter me, shading me from the sun as he curves his body around mine. "Everyone here knows you're being punished right now. All eyes are on you. They pretend to sip their drinks or watch the waves, but you're the real show. They can see I'm spanking you, but I won't let anyone see what's mine."

"So, they can't see my ass but they can see everything else?" I groan. "Great. Like that's fine."

He runs a finger along my crack, sending shivers down my spine. "You think I'd let them see your bare ass? That's the whole point, isn't it? What this bathing suit shows is for my eyes only. Let's see if I can convince you to change."

Groaning, I wriggle my hips, unsure if I want to get away or feel his hands on me more. The sensation of the heat of his skin against mine, the feel of his strong muscles moving beneath me, the stir of his cock against my belly.

The eyes of the people.

It's equal parts humiliating and thrilling and I don't understand it, a pool of arousal slickening between my thighs. Am I turned on or dying of shame? Both.

He slaps my ass again, not enough to hurt, just to sting, to wake up every nerve ending in my skin, making me whine and roll my hips against him.

"Stop," I say, but my words are weak, laced with desire. "Stop."

"Are you ready to go to your room and change into something more reasonable?" His finger dips between my thighs, and I moan as he plays in the slickness.

"Maybe," I say. "Depending on what else we'll be doing in that room."

"My little girl wants her ass spanked and her pussy fucked. Doesn't she?" I gasp as he shoves a finger inside me, delicious friction running up the walls of my sex.

The truth comes out in a whimper, his finger stroking me inside. "Yes. Please." I don't even care about the people on the beach any longer. I just want more of him inside me.

He gives a laugh and I feel it rumble from his chest through my entire body. He snaps my bathing suit bottoms back into place. I go to stand but he doesn't allow that, does he? No, he ends my punishment with the further humiliation of standing up and tossing me over his shoulder like a rag doll, my ass on full display, the tiny triangle barely covering anything.

I pummel his back, strong with muscles and warm and tan from the sun, with my fists. "You put me down right now, Liam Bachman."

"Settle down." He gives my ass a sharp spank as he carries me up the sandy shore to the grass. "Bet you wish you were wearing a more modest suit right about now—your ass has handprints all over it..."

"Ugh!" I groan, giving up and flopping over his back, bouncing against him as he carries me across the beach. Over the threshold to the mansion, past the staff, up the stairs, and into my room.

He tosses me down on the bed. I've had the entire walk to plan my speech, a long lecture on equality between man and woman and how barbaric his actions were on the beach but before I can open my mouth, his is on mine, locking us in a heated kiss. He slides his knee up along my thigh and...

Bzzzzzzzzzzzzzzzzzz...

His knee is... vibrating against my leg? I mean, I know I turn him on but—oh my God! I come to my senses, realizing what's happening.

I pull away from his kiss, pushing against his chest. "Ah. Hang on a minute. Can you go and come back? I just need a minute—"

One look from his dark eyes and I swallow up my words. He arches a brow. "What is that?"

I reach my hand down, pressing at the covers, hoping to hit the button he accidentally hit, turning it off.

His dark eyes find mine, his voice stern. "Babygirl."

Shame fills me as his hands slip under the covers, searching for the toy.

"Nooo..." This can't be happening. It's too humiliating. He does not need to know about my toy. There's no way in his little charred marshmallow heart he's going to find that vibrator, be a gentleman, and let this go.

He holds the purple vibrator up like a trophy. "Was someone frustrated last night?"

I bury my face in my hands, groaning.

He flips the switch, leaving the bed. "You have any other goodies in here?"

"No. Don't!" But I seem glued to the bed in fear, and I don't get up to stop him.

I hear the nightstand drawer opening. The hum of the little clitoral vibrator.

He flashes me the most wicked grin. "Be right back."

He disappears into the bathroom, leaving me hot and bothered and totally embarrassed, laying on the bed in nothing but this stupid string bikini that started it all. I can't decide if I love it or hate it right now.

And he's back, one toy in each of his hands. He stands at the end of the bed, looming over me looking like a Greek god right about now with his sculpted muscles and bronze tan. A dark lock of hair has fallen over one eye.

"Now. Which one of these should I punish you with first?"

LIAM

HER EYES GO WIDE AS SHE STARES AT THE WEAPONS I HOLD IN MY hands. "Well, babygirl. What'll it be?" I click on the full-sized vibrator with the awesome little nub meant for her ass. "If you don't choose, I'll pick for you. I think this one would do nicely, filling you while I finish what I started on the beach."

She creeps back on the bed, scooting toward the headboard. "You already spanked me."

"Not enough. I get the feeling you still have a disobedient streak running through you."

Her full lips pout, making my point. She slides her pretty legs up, bending her knees, showing me the fullness of her ass and hips. She sticks out her breasts, points of beauty showcased in thin triangles of deep blue fabric. Thin straps wind around her back and over her shoulders in an intricate fashion. She grabs the end of the tie around her neck, twirling it between her forefinger and her thumb, teasing me.

"Do I?" my pet purrs. "Doesn't sound like me."

Fuck.

One breath later, I've dropped the vibrators on the bed and I'm on her, tearing those tiny, ridiculous bathing suit bottoms off her. I toss them to the floor, taking in the gorgeous view of her waxed pussy. I thrust a finger in her just to get off on seeing how wet I make her. She's soaked, so responsive to me.

Her legs part, her back arches. "Make me come." But she's not getting off that easy.

I grab her waist, throwing her over my lap as I sit on the edge of the bed. She's splayed over my lap, her bare legs hanging down, nothing hiding her skin from me but a few strings on her back. I push a finger in her again, making her buck against me. I take my fingers from her, using the slickness on my fingers to lube her asshole, readying her for the vibrating nub of the toy.

It's sexy and fun but I'm rough, wanting her to have no doubt in her mind I'm to be obeyed, even if it's something as simple as changing a bathing suit if I find it inappropriate.

I shove her legs apart, thrusting the first half of the vibrator inside her, cranking it up to medium-high.

She gives a squeal, her hips bucking against me, making my cock grow hard. I smooth a hand over her ass, then raise my palm, bringing it down in a hard spank. The spank makes her moan. I push the toy all the way inside her, pressing the vibrating nub inside of her rosebud ring of tight ass muscles.

The toy now fully in her, she cries out, "Oh my God!"

"You like playing with your toy when I'm not here?" I spank her right cheek, a beautiful red handprint rising on her skin.

Her protest is a moan. "Nooo..."

"I think you're lying. I think you were lying in your bed last night, thinking of me while you played with your toys."

"Uhn..." she cries. "Okay, okay. Yes! Are you happy?"

"There's that sassy attitude." I spank her again, hard and fast, my open palm spanking her right cheek, then left. "The same one you had on the beach earlier. The same one that got you over my lap in the first place. I'm going to keep you here till you learn your lesson."

"And what is that?" A whine rises in her throat. "How to come so hard I explode?"

I chuckle. "I won't let that happen. But I might let you beg."

I pull the toy out of her.

Her body goes rigid. Frozen. She's a tight line of muscles over my lap.

"What"—her head turns slowly over her shoulder, her eyes wide, her mouth gaping— "are you doing?"

"Stopping," I say.

"Why?"

"I want to hear you beg."

"Oh my God," she whines. "Liam. Please. Put that thing back in me."

"Are you going to be a good girl? And do as I say?" I ask.

She bites her lip, thinking. Clearly this is a difficult concept for her. "Um..."

I give her ass another smack that makes her jump.

"Yes! Okay? Yes. I'll be good."

Shoving her legs apart, I line the vibrator up with her entrance, turn it on, and push it fully inside of her, letting the nub go inside her ass at the same time.

Her hands grasp at the covers, looking for something to anchor her to this world. Her hips move back and forth, fucking the toy as she lays over my lap.

I love this, the power I have over her, the fight to draw pleasure from her beautiful body, the way she responds to me, wanting more and resisting me all at once. She comes, hard, her body curling around mine, shuddering as I tear the toy from her.

15

E *milia*

MY MOUTH GAPES LIKE A FISH ON THE SHORE, NO WORDS COMING OUT. My core aches, my sex and ass clenching and pulsing as the final waves of orgasm tear through me.

I'm falling apart, my body like jelly, but he's not finished with me yet.

He flips me off his lap, tossing me onto the bed on my belly. He comes behind me, the fronts of his thighs pressing against the backs of mine. A hand slides over my shoulder, down my chest. His fingers slip over the silky material of the suit. He pinches my hard nipple between his fingers.

"You like the suit so much, leave the top on," he says. "I like the way your nipples feel in it."

He grabs my breast, squeezing. His hand dips into the triangle of my top, the pad of his thumb stroking my nipple.

My palms are damp as I grab at the covers, clutching the fabric. Is that... buzzing?

A soft hum fills the room but different this time. He's got the clitoral stimulator, a toy I haven't been brave enough to use on myself yet. Oh God.

"I—I can't." My voice shakes, my knees weak, still recovering from the first orgasm. Can I handle a second one?

His fingers reach around my waist, dipping down inside my sex. "So wet for me, babygirl." He strokes my clit, rubbing circles around it.

My hips rotate against his hand, circling the other direction. I feel him shove his suit down behind me, freeing his cock, the head brushing against my ass cheeks.

"Spread those pretty legs, baby."

I spread my legs.

"Further."

I slide my feet apart, wanting him, yet at the same time thinking I can't take any more. He moves the vibrator between my legs, and at the very same moment the buzzing silicone suction cup nestles around my aching bud, he fills me with his cock, thick and hard and glorious as it momentarily lifts the wanting ache inside me.

He turns up the vibrator, a shocking bolt of pleasure bursting through me, my sex tightening around him. He pulls back, thrusting his hips forward, impaling me hard with his cock as he turns up the speed of the vibrator.

"Liam!" I can't think, I can't speak, other than to scream his name. "Liam!"

My heart rate rises. My temperature skyrockets, heat flashing over my skin. Perspiration prickles under my arms and at the back of my neck.

My sex swells, my clit throbbing in the toy as another orgasm ricochets through me. He fucks me hard, again and again, his cock building tension in my core while the toy teases my clit. I can't take more. This is his punishment, to overstimulate me, to throw me over the edge of the cliff, so undone I can only say his name.

He's taking my body, making it his because I know after this, I am ruined.

There will never be another man for me.

"Liam, please." I clutch at the blankets, my ass moving back, greedy for more of his cock, even though I can't take it. Another climax hits my clit, bursting through me, making my sex clench around him.

He builds a rhythm, thrusting his hips forward, pulling them back, filling me then retreating, the friction inside me building but also being overcome by waves of climax reverberating from my clit.

"Liam!" I gasp. "Liam! I can't take anymore!"

Just when I think I'm about to pass out, he grabs my hips, giving a low growl as he brings me back against him hard, filling me with his hot cum. It fills me and I can feel his sex pulsing as he releases his pleasure inside me.

He leans down, trailing a line of gentle kisses along my lower back. His tenderness surprises me. I lay across the bed, my cheek damp against the covers, spent.

He slaps my ass. "Now wear something pretty that doesn't show so much skin. And watch that mouth of yours—don't make me spank you at the ball. Although I'm sure everyone is hoping for an encore."

Heat rises in my cheeks at the mention of another public spanking. "You're infuriating. You know that?" I toss a pillow at him, missing him. "Now get out."

He stands in the doorway, arms crossed over his chest. "Say please."

"Ugh! Are you serious?"

"I told you how I feel about rudeness."

I throw the pillows one after the other.

"Please. Get. Out."

He leaves, laughing as he goes.

I shower, my knees like jelly after all the things he did to me. I throw on a robe, gather my things, and stomp over to the bright pink B-Hive to get ready for the Springtime Ball with the other girls.

His voice lingers in my mind. *Don't make me spank you at the ball. Although I'm sure everyone is hoping for an encore.* It's making my skin hot and my temper rise. I drag my brush through my hair, tugging on it when it gets tangled in a knot.

"Slow down!" Jules comes running over, taking the brush from my hand. "You're going to tear your hair out."

"Did you see what he did to me on the beach?" I say. "I'm so angry. How can I show my face at the ball tonight, knowing everyone there got a good look at my bare ass!"

Jules gives a low whistle. "*Sooo* yeah, wasn't on the beach this morning, I was too busy making sure that everything was set up perfectly for tonight... but I *may* have heard something about the whole 'Liam going crazy over the bikini' thing? But the way he bent over you totally covered everything, I swear. No one saw anything, as far as I heard, well, except for you over his lap, your legs kicking."

"Oh God." I bury my face in my hands in shame as she gently detangles my hair with the brush.

"But I wasn't there. I heard from Hannah, who heard from Sasha, who, you know... kinda saw the whole thing?"

"Can a person die of embarrassment? I literally think I'm going to die," I say.

"If it makes you feel any better, Sasha said it was crazy hot. Like, she made it sound like she wished she was the one over Liam's lap on that beach. And this should really make you feel better." She leans over my shoulder.

I peek between my fingers, catching her eye in the mirror. "What?"

"It's happened to all us girls." Jules shrugs, a cat-that-got-the-cream smile on her pretty face. "It's kinda part of the lifestyle. Usually happens when we test them and go a bit too far. That's when the spanking goes public."

I try to picture prim Jules being spanked in public. "That hasn't happened to you, though, has it?"

"Oh, yes. Let me tell you. Sasha's husband Carter spanked her at our dance club, Gotcha's, in New York city one night before they were even married."

Sasha, I can see someone wanting to spank her. But prim and proper Jules?

"What about you, though?" I ask.

"I had one too many margaritas at our Cinco de Mayo party. Preston tried to cut me off, but I started sneaking them. They were just so good! They even had this pretty liquor that made them blue. And I was in one of those can't-be-told-what-to-do moods. Tequila has a way of aiding me in bad decision-making. Anyway. He caught me and right there in front of everyone in the rooftop bar, tipped me right over his lap."

"Jules. Seriously?"

"Yes. I switched to water after that, and I don't think I sat down on May sixth."

I think of the modest one-pieces he'd had his staff order me. How much I wanted to tempt him, to make him want me. "I guess I crossed that line."

A naughty glint flashes through her gaze. "Fun, isn't it?"

"It was a little fun." I giggle, thinking of him ripping my top off and burying himself in me. "Especially afterwards."

Jules dresses me in a shimmering yellow gown, the perfect shade for my coloring, of course. The neckline is high, covering my breasts. I'm not taking any chances tonight. I wear my hair up, thanking Sasha for braiding it, then coiling the braids together and pinning them in place. I wear the gold hoops and some strappy sandal heels. I feel perfect, excited, ready to join everyone for my first ball. But as we get closer to the event, I start fuming again, just thinking of him and his public punishment.

How. Dare. He.

Sure, the Beauties' fiancés and husbands punish them, but Liam is just my... what is he? Bodyguard? Friend? No, he's too grumpy to be a friend. Whatever he is, he has no right to take such liberties with me, and I'm going to tell him so.

By the time he comes to escort me, I'm ready for a fight.

He looks too damn good in that tux, his hair slicked back. A wicked smile spreads across his face as he offers me his arm. "Such a pretty girl. It's a shame you're spoiling that gown with such an angry face."

I take his arm, hissing, "If you don't like my face, don't look at it."

He makes a *tsk tsk* sound. "You're pouting."

"I'm not pouting. I'm pissed off."

"You didn't like your spanking on the beach? Or your punishment that followed? You could have fooled me, the way you were screaming my name." He smirks and I want to scratch the smile off his handsome face.

He knows how wet his punishments make me.

"You spanked me. In public. In front of your family," I hiss.

He shrugs. "You deserved it. You disobeyed me. You never should have come out on the beach in a suit I didn't approve of."

"You have to approve of my clothing now? You're not even my boyfriend."

"But you are under my care."

"Not for long," I say. "The second we get back—"

Our banter ends. I feel the air around us change in an instant, filling with tension. He turns to me, grabbing my shoulders, forcing my gaze to meet his. "What do you think is going to happen when we get back to Italy? That you'll waltz into your home, and all will be forgiven? You're being naïve. Sure, your father fears me and won't hit you again, but you'll be facing another marriage and I have a feeling your father will punish you with his choice of groom. The older the better. I'm sure there's a man out there with plenty of money who won't care you're not a virgin."

"Are you being serious right now?" I shrug him off, walking away.

He keeps pace with me. "Trust me. You humiliated your father when you didn't show up for that wedding. He will, in turn, humiliate you. His next pick will make John Romano, who is a good man, by the way, look like a teenager."

"He wouldn't do that to me." But as I say the words, I know he would. I see my father, rage etched in the lines of his face.

"You'll have to come back to my house. Live under my roof. Or run. Only to be tracked down and found by men you won't want to know. Men that will snatch you up just to say they've had a taste of the Accardi princess. Without my protection—"

The hopelessness of my situation settles around me like a cloud, my anger dissipating. "I'm nothing."

"No." He holds my shoulders tight. "You're *everything*. And men will want you."

I let his words settle around me.

His voice softens. "What did you think would happen when we leave here?"

"I don't know..."

"You're so naïve," he says again.

"I'd rather be naïve than cruel," I spit back.

His tone softens. "I'm not cruel. I'm just telling you like it is."

I take it down a notch. "So, what are my choices? Live with you the rest of my life?"

"Or find a suitable husband who will protect you from both your father's wrath and the Romanos' revenge."

"God, I hate being a woman sometimes."

"It's a shame because you're very good at it." He gives an almost-laugh. "I swear I nearly came the moment I saw you on that beach."

"Came?" I say. "I thought you were going to have a heart attack, you were so mad."

"I could have done both."

I have to laugh at that. I go to say something back, but I feel a cool hand on my shoulder.

I turn my head to find Charlie's concerned eyes. "Emilia, Liam. Rockland and Tess would like to see you now. They're in the library."

Ice forms in my belly and on my tongue. My fate hangs in the frigid air around me.

"Thank you." Liam nods to Charlie, then turns to me. "I'll take care of it. It's my fault. I'm the one who came to your room that night."

"I made that crazy deal with you," I say, finally able to speak.

He takes my hand and though fear and nerves surround me, I feel safe. His eyes catch mine. "We're in this together. Let's go."

The room is deep green and dark wood, the walls lined with books. A place I'd find cozy if such an important meeting wasn't taking place. Rockland, a massive man with cropped dark hair and the deepest tan I've ever seen, stands by a fireplace, a roaring fire crackling inside. A beautiful redhead dressed in a cream gown stands by his side, a scowl on her gorgeous face.

They exchange greetings with us and make introductions. I can barely speak but manage handshakes and pleasantries. Rockland places a soft kiss on my cheek.

We take a seat at a small card table in the library with four seats, one at each edge of the square.

Rockland speaks directly to me. "You broke off the engagement your father arranged and, in the process, disrespected an important ally of ours. We've been working with both the Russo and the Romano families to establish dominance of Northern and Southern Italy. We have an agreement with the Romano family."

Tess turns to Liam. "And you, Liam, tarnished the Bachman name by stealing her away with no real claim to her or plan to make her your own."

Make her your own? The words don't sit right with me. Especially coming from a powerful woman.

"You're talking about me as if I'm an object," I say to Tess. "Or not even in the room."

"This," says Tess, "is mafia life, Emilia. It's time for you to grow up and accept your place in this world. Only then will we speak to you and not of you."

Her biting words snap my tongue in two, my face burning with shame.

"We don't want a war," Rockland says. "Is that what the two of you want?"

Liam answers for both of us. "No."

Rockland looks to Liam. "We can tell the Accardis and the Romanos that we've made our decision, that what you did was in our plan. And we can fight the inevitable war that will come our way. Or we can tell them that you and Emilia had a change of heart. That you are happy to outbid John Romano for her hand in marriage and put in a fair dowry to smooth things over with her father. Then, we give Romano what he wants to settle him down: access to one of the brownstones in New York to sell the Romano Estates wines out of. A front, of course, to help them establish some ties in the States."

Tess stares at Liam, ignoring me. "It's your call, Liam."

I want to shout the question burning in my mind. *Don't I get a say in this?!* But Tess's words still have my tongue. She's right. At some point, I need to accept this life that I was born into.

I must lift my crown as the Accardi princess and wear it proudly.

I turn to Liam. "I respect your decision."

He's as shocked by my words as I am.

"What do you want?" he asks me, doling me a surprise of his own. "You make the final decision."

I hadn't expected that...

I thought he'd play his big man card, demanding we do it his way, that he would lead, and I follow. I was almost counting on it, really, to be spared the hard decision and have him decide my fate for me. Then, however this thing ends up, I could be the victim, the one who was forced, without a say in the decision.

But now... I have to make the choice.

Tess looks right at me. "It's time to accept your place, Mafia Princess."

I could wallow in self-pity, telling myself I'm not something to be sold, that my marriage never should have been arranged in the first place, but Tess's words stay strong in my mind.

It's time to accept your place, Mafia Princess.

The Beauties' faces play in my mind's eye. I am sure of one thing. Putting them in danger is not an option.

I'm facing the consequences of our actions.

I'm donning my crown.

My words come clear and true. "I don't want war."

"Then there's only one solution." Liam looks right at me, his dark eyes piercing me all the way down in my soul. "We'll be married. Tomorrow."

16

L *iam*

I KNEW IT WOULD COME TO THIS, BUT THE REALITY HITS ME LIKE A punch in the chest all the same, air leaving my lungs, my legs unsteady. It takes everything in me to control my voice, to keep it even, steady for her.

"We'll be married. Tomorrow."

Emilia's eyes are on me.

She needs my strength, even though I feel weak in the knees.

Emilia has that look of shock and fear, like when our headlights shone on her face when I found her running on the road that night. Tess's face sings with relief. Rockland's face gives away nothing.

Rockland nods. "Fine. That gives us tonight to work out contracts and payments with Accardi and Romano."

And that gives me tonight to tell her about Emily. I need time to tell her the truth about me.

We go back up to the room, a heady silence between us. It's difficult to wrap our minds around what's just been decided.

"Emilia. I have to talk to you."

She's dazed, her fingers trembling in mine.

I guide her to the balcony. "Wait here."

I go back to the room, to the built-in bar, pulling a chilled pinot grigio from the wine fridge. She's going to need a drink for this. It'll be hard for her to hear my story, but I won't marry her without her knowing it.

I won't marry her without her knowing the other me.

Liam Black.

I pour her a generous glass, and a whiskey for myself. One drink in each hand, I stand in the center of the room, taking in the vision that is her. The glass doors are open, the night air swirling around us. She stands with her back to me, staring out over the sea. The hem of her yellow-gold dress flutters around her heels, moving with the breeze.

Her hair is coiled up in an elaborate updo. She's wearing the earrings I gave her. She's as perfect as a painting, standing here. If her dress was white, she could be a bride, ready for her wedding day.

As I step out onto the balcony, I can almost picture it. Emilia and me, married, visiting the Parish, drinking under the stars.

This is us.

I hand her the wineglass. The tips of her fingers graze mine as she takes it. "Thank you. I've never had white wine before."

"I think you're going to love it. Take a sip."

She tilts the glass back, trying it. A smile shines on her face. "Delicious."

I hold up my tumbler. "Here's to..."

What to toast to? Bad decisions leading to forced marriages?

The salty sea breeze blows by, heady with springtime grass and the scent of jasmine growing in the garden. Spring. A time of renewal. Po's words come to me.

Maybe I *can* do the stuff.

"Here's to new beginnings." I raise my glass to hers.

"To new beginnings. Cheers." She gives my glass a delicate clink with hers.

She turns back to the sea, sipping her wine, lost in thought. I stand beside her on the balcony, watching the waves as they crash to the shore.

"Growing up it was my mom and me and my four brothers. I was the oldest. By the time I was fifteen I had a job after school and a second on the weekends to help make ends meet. But the town we lived in, there wasn't much money to go around and even with me working part-time and my mom working full-time, we were still broke. I had to get out of there. To make something of myself so I could, in turn, get my brothers out."

"That's a lot of responsibility." Her gaze searches mine.

"I tried my best, for all of us. God, did I try. I went to college. Worked two jobs. Lived off ramen and fruit and sent every penny I could home. Then, I met a woman. Sarah."

Her shoulders tense.

"We became... attached. I wouldn't call it love, but we moved in together. We were both struggling financially, and it just made more sense. One rent, one utility bill. Things were going okay. Good, even. Then, she got pregnant."

Emilia turns to me, her eyes wide, but she stays quiet, just listening.

"I was shocked at first. Scared as hell. I didn't know how to be a dad. I mean, I helped out with my brothers, but they weren't babies and I didn't raise them. This, this was different. I tried to talk her into adopting the baby out. We could barely afford to feed ourselves. How were we going to pay for diapers?"

"Right. That's a lot." She takes a sip of wine.

"But then, the baby was born. A little girl. The nurse handed her to me. She looked right at me, cooed, and grabbed my finger. I was gone. I knew, no matter what happened in this world, I would love and protect that little girl. And no one," my voice breaks, "would ever take her from me."

Emilia puts her hand on my shoulder. "What happened?"

"We went home from the hospital, the three of us. We tried to make it work, but I knew something was off with Sarah. One day, she took off. Left a note saying she wasn't ready to be a mother and not to contact her."

Emilia looks out over the sea. "You were on your own with a baby."

"Yes. But I didn't care. As long as I had my little girl and she had me, I knew the two of us would be fine."

"But it wasn't fine," she says gently. "Was it?"

I shake my head, not trusting myself to speak. How can I say the words out loud? How can I tell her what happened next?

"I hated to ever leave her, but I had to work. I took a job working nights so that I would only be gone while the baby was sleeping.

There was a woman in the apartment above us, Ms. Jenkins. She agreed to watch the baby while I worked. I didn't know it at the time, but Ms. Jenkins wasn't... healthy. She suffered from seizures that would sometimes leave her blacked out for hours. I didn't know about her health at the time."

"Oh no." Emilia keeps her eyes trained on mine.

"One night Ms. Jenkins was watching the baby for me while I was working. When I was coming home, I heard the sirens before I even made it to our block. My heart went cold in my chest. I knew something was wrong. When I got to the building, it was surrounded by firetrucks. Smoke was billowing out of all the third-floor windows."

"Ms. Jenkin's floor?" she asks.

"Yes."

Her hand flutters over her heart. "Oh my God."

I spare her the rest of the details. Me pushing past the police, then the firemen, running to the third floor. A fireman, fully dressed in his garb, his helmet on his head, walking toward me through the smoke, carrying a tiny bundle in his arms.

I remember thinking *that can't be Emily. That can't be my girl.*

My throat grows tight, my voice thick as I say, "Later, I found out about Ms. Jenkins and her seizures. She had one that night. That's why she didn't get them out. They both died of smoke inhalation."

A moment of heavy silence hangs between us.

"I'm so, so sorry." She dabs at the tears forming in the corners of her eyes. "May I ask your baby's name?"

I choke on the precious word. "Emily."

"Emily." Her word is a whisper. "Emily." Her eyes find mine. "I see. That must be... hard. To have an Emilia in your life now."

"Not hard, it just brought up those feelings..."

"And fears," she says.

"Yes." I nod. "Fears."

"I understand." She rubs my back, her hands making circles over my suit jacket.

Emilia is so special, so sweet. The way she listens, the sound of her soothing voice when she speaks... she lets me talk about the past in a way I've not been able to.

The way she is, the way she makes me feel, it lets me continue my story.

"After that, I went into a dark place. I couldn't eat. Couldn't sleep." I give a scoff of a laugh. "But I could drink. That, I could do."

I take a sip of whiskey, remembering the way it used to make me feel. Heady and light, taking the pain away for just a moment, then waking to the same nightmare every morning, only with a raging headache, my body feeling like it'd been dragged through the gutter.

"I can imagine. A loss like that." Her voice goes distant. "It wrecks you."

"That's right," I say. "You lost your mother."

"It's not the same as losing a child, I'm sure. I'm just saying, I kind of know that heartache you talk about. The one that made you drink. Mine makes me run."

"There's no contest over grief," I say. "We're all losers. I'm sure your mother's death was incredibly painful."

"It was more her absence that was painful. I have a feeling you know what I mean." She gives me a soft look.

I remember how my arms felt so strangely empty for the first full year after Emily died, her perfect, familiar weight missing from them.

"I know exactly what you mean," I say.

"And you joined the mafia after that?" she asks.

"Yes. I wanted to live in a world where darkness and pain weren't masked. Where wars were real. A life where death was a risk. I wanted to feel again. I met one of the Bachmans. Bronson. He was taking over as head of the family at the time. He was young. So young. But he just had this power about him. He walked in a room and men respected him. I couldn't go on like I was. I needed to end Liam Black. To reinvent myself."

"And so, you became Liam Bachman."

My hand goes to the tattoo that covers my heart. "Yes. The Brotherhood saved me. Without them..." My throat closes up.

She gives me a moment. "And you brought your brothers from home into the fold?"

"Yes, but not until later when I was more established. I started small, just running simple tasks for the family. They trusted me more and more. Soon, I was one of their hitmen. Taking out anyone who stood in the way of building our empire. I proved myself over the years, slowly accruing more and more men below me. When Rockland took over for Bronson, he sent me here. Rockland had been working with Vincent Russo, in Southern Italy. He saw their union as a chance to expand. That's when I got all four of my younger blood brothers to join me. Including Cannon. The dirty little bastard is running the kink club."

"I remember meeting him," she says. "At the speed dating. When you tried to pawn me off on one of your brothers. He's handsome."

"They all are."

"But none as handsome as you." She wraps an arm around my neck, reaching up to kiss my cheek. Her lips brush against my skin. Tiny sparks of electricity rush down my spine at her light touch.

"I don't know about that. But that's my story. And here I am."

"Heading up the Northern branch of the family." She brushes her fingers over my jaw. "The king of the mafia."

"Exactly. And tomorrow, you become my queen."

She holds up her glass. "Cheers to that."

"Cheers." I clink my glass against hers and she smiles.

But her smile doesn't quite reach her eyes.

Is it the heaviness of my story that doesn't allow for her happiness, or is it that she's having to marry?

Or does she not smile because she's marrying... me?

EMILIA

TOMORROW, I MAKE MY VOW TO THE KING.

I'm no longer the battered and broken princess, living not alone but completely lonely in a crumbling mansion. I will make my vow and become a queen.

I will live on a beautiful estate surrounded by wealth, my view no longer the dark forest but the stunning aquamarine of the lake and the snowy peaks of the mountains.

The Beauties will be my friends. Strong women will be an exciting new part of my life. After this trip, I've come to believe that women need other women in their lives to be whole.

It's all going to be mine.

So why do I feel so empty inside?

My groom lusts after me. There is no mistaking the desire in his eyes whenever he looks my way. Heat radiates from his hands whenever he touches me.

He wants me.

But he doesn't want this marriage.

He's too scarred from the loss in his past. He doesn't want to risk being hurt again. He doesn't want to be bound to another Emily. The name Emily is just too close to Emilia to not bring up his pain, time and time again.

I understand why he doesn't want to love again. Why he doesn't want to risk opening himself up to someone. What he went through was horrible.

I can understand, but I can't help wishing it wasn't this way.

That instead, on my wedding day, my groom wanted to marry me. Somehow over the past few weeks, I've gotten over my fear of men, my fear of being tied to one.

A husband no longer seems like a death sentence.

Not all men are my enemy.

I've shifted my loyalties from my family... to him. He will protect me. He's already shown he's willing to make a huge sacrifice for me. From now on, my loyalties lie with him.

I want to marry him.

I just wish he wanted to marry me.

17

E *milia*

I TELL LIAM I HAVE A HEADACHE, CHOOSING TO SLEEP ALONE FOR THE last time, my mind fuzzy with all that's going on. The morning comes quickly and I'm summoned early, before sunrise, to the B-Hive, told to wear just my underthings and a robe.

Any sadness I feel about my groom dragging his feet to the altar disappears the moment the pink mansion comes into view. The Beauties wrap me in their arms, pulling me into the main hall, their giggles infectious. I can't believe I get to be one of them.

My fuzzy pink-slippered feet come to a stop as I look around the hall. It's been decorated as if there's going to be a party.

Streamers made of long, pink feathers hang from the chandelier, draping from the center of the room to the corners. A table is spread with all kinds of goodies and treats, chocolate-covered strawberries and pink and green macarons. A bubble machine releases iridescent rainbow bubbles of different sizes into the air around us.

Ella, the Beauty with long dark hair, takes my arm. "It's last minute, we know, but that's no excuse not to have a bachelorette party. We've got drinks and pastries and chocolates, but nothing too heavy since we've got the Spring brunch."

Jules follows close behind. "It'll have to be shorter than we'd like. We've only got a few hours to party and get you ready for the wedding. Then, a quick ceremony on the beach and we'll celebrate your marriage at the brunch."

"But don't worry. In a few weeks we'll fly you to New York for a proper reception. Dinner and drinks and all-night dancing." Sasha gives a business-like nod.

Jules quickly adds, "And the ceremony you have to go through to become an official Bachman."

Oh yeah, the secret ceremony I've heard about, just for the Bachman wives. Let's hear more. "Ah... can you tell me a bit more about that?"

Jules shakes her head. "Nope. Just focus on today, babe. That's all you need to do. We'll have a simple wedding, a little party, then send you home."

Ella gently nudges me with her elbow. "So you and your husband can celebrate."

Sasha waggles her brows. "Privately."

The women fall into another fit of giggles.

"Seriously? Sometimes I feel like I'm surrounded by schoolgirls." Jules laughs, taking my hand. "Come with me."

She leads me to a massive hot-pink cushioned chair that looks like a throne. It's set up in the center of the room, dozens of brightly colored packages surrounding it, the paper shiny, the bows massive and glittery.

"Is this all for me?" I fall into the deep cushions of the chair.

"Of course!"

"But how did you pull this off? We just found out we were marrying last night and then you all had the ball and—"

"We stayed up all night," Jules says. "It was our pleasure."

"How are you still awake?" I ask.

Sasha joins us, a tiny white cup on a saucer in each hand. She gives one to me. "That's what espresso is for."

"Thank you." I take a tiny sip of the bitter coffee. Whoa. Not for me. But I need the caffeine, so I sip at the cup.

I've got a big day ahead of me.

The women, some dressed in their gowns from last night, some dressed in leggings and tees, others in cute matching pajama sets, surround me.

They drink coffee or mimosas, handing me bits of chocolate in between gifts of jewelry, purses, shoes. All chosen according to Jules' color specifications. I love every item. I hold a soft green leather pouch to my cheek, inhaling the earthy scent.

The chocolate melts on my tongue, sweet and creamy, powering me through as I open the presents. The next package holds the under-garments I'm to wear today for my wedding. If you could call them garments. Nude bra and thong, made of the thinnest fabric. The Beauties believe underwear should only be seen when that's all that a woman is wearing. It absolutely cannot be visible beneath a gown.

Then comes the lingerie I wear after the wedding. A tremble of nerves shoots through me as I peel back the lid to reveal a gorgeous, peach-colored scalloped lace two-piece set, mid-rise panties with a longline bralette. "It's so pretty."

"And you're going to look stunning in it." Ella smiles.

Charlie comes dancing over, a long white garment bag in her hand, singing the "Wedding March" as she goes. "Dum, da, da dum! Dum, da, da dum!" She stops just before me, bowing deep at the waist like a servant to a queen.

"What have you got there?" But as I ask, a torrent of butterflies takes flight in my stomach. I know exactly what's in that bag she holds.

My dress.

My *wedding* dress.

"Go ahead. Open it." She's positively glowing. "It's yours."

I look up into her open, smiling face and smile back. Standing from the throne, I take the zipper between my forefinger and thumb. My fingers are shaking too badly. The espresso? I look to Charlie. "Can you?"

"Of course." She leans in, whispering in my ear, a warm hand on my forearm to steady me. "It's normal. To be nervous."

"Thanks." I sink back down into the throne.

Sasha comes to her and helps her free the gown from the bag. A long, pale ivory-colored silk gown. They immediately pull me from the throne, carting me off to their dressing room to try it on.

The neckline is high, like the yellow gown. Lace like a collar that ties behind the neck to hold the delicate fabric up. There is no back to the dress, the silk showing back up just at the dip above my waist.

"I'm sorry, but you have a runner's body. I'm not going to *not* show it off. Look at your back. It's gorgeous."

I look over my shoulder, seeking my reflection in the mirror. She's not wrong. I look beautiful, but strong.

"I love it." My voice is a whisper. "I love it."

They finish getting me ready, laughing and talking as they put on their own gowns, doing one another's hair and makeup.

There's a knock on the door.

"Wait here." Charlie dashes to the door to see who it is.

There's a staff member, whispering words to her. Charlie shakes her head. I think I can hear her say, "Absolutely not."

The staff speaks more quickly, their hands waving in the air. Whatever they're talking about, they're upset. Their eyes meet mine.

Charlie crosses her arms over her chest. "No. No way. No men come in the B-Hive and absolutely no grooms seeing their bride before—"

The door shoves open.

There, on the threshold of the dressing room, stands Liam, taking my breath away with his almost inhuman good looks. His black tux, his hair gelled back, a rogue lock hanging over one of his dark eyes.

He steps into the room. "Emilia."

Our eyes lock and hold.

Somehow, it's just the two of us in this room, even though it's filled with women. Soon, we are the only two left. One by one, the Beauties file out, making excuses about taking their seats for the wedding.

My breaths come faster in my chest, my heart pounding. He's here and his presence, it just does something to me, makes my knees weak and my heart pound and when I look at him, I know I'm looking at my future.

In just a few minutes... he'll be my husband.

He holds out a large, square, black velvet jewelry box. "I have a gift for you."

"For me?" I say. "But I've been spoiled all day."

"Not by me." He kisses my cheek. It's a cool, sweet kiss and it calms me.

I flip the lid open. Inside the velvet is a necklace made of black pearls with matching pearl earrings. I lift the necklace from the box, holding it up to the light. The black color has hints of greens and blues and purples. "They're so beautiful. I've never seen anything like it."

"Tahitian South Sea pearls. Let me put them on you."

I turn.

His fingers are warm, the black pearls cold against the silk of my dress as he clasps the necklace behind my neck while I put the earrings in. I like the weight of the necklace against my chest. I reach up, stroking the precious beads.

"Thank you."

He leans down over me, his cheek against mine. A smile curls at my lips at the warmth of his closeness. I love when he holds me like this, standing behind me, sheltering me in his chest, his arms.

He fingers the pearls. "They look beautiful on you. Just like I knew they would." His fingers dip down, gliding over my clavicle, dragging over the swell of my breasts, dipping down between them.

Cold creeps in. I freeze.

I reach up, taking his fingers in mine. I turn around to face him, offering a weak smile. "Sorry. I just... I don't like that."

"You don't like when I touch your breasts?" He pulls back.

I squeeze his hand in mine. "No. I love that. I love when you touch me. Everywhere. It's just this one thing. I have a funny reaction to you... touching my cleavage." I quickly fill in the words, not wanting to insult him. "Not just you, anyone. If anyone touches me like that—"

"What do you mean, anyone?" His dark brows knit together. "Who else has touched you like this?"

Shit.

Double shit.

"That's not what I meant." I try to cover my tracks. "I just mean, I wouldn't want anyone to touch me—"

"Emilia. We're getting married. Now. We're past secrets. I don't want anything between us. Tell me. Who touched you?"

Heat from shame rises in my face and I need to look away. "It's just, sometimes, if I wear a dress, or something low-cut like a tank top, one of my brothers..."

How do I explain what Antonio does to torment me? How the tops of my breasts tempt him, and he touches me in ways that don't quite cross a line but edge up to it, constantly?

He pulls my chin up, trapping it between his forefinger and his thumb. "I see it's hard for you to talk about this, but you need to tell me. Now."

The words tumble from my lips. "Antonio. He does that. Runs his finger over the tops of my breasts and dips it into my cleavage."

Heat pulsates from his eyes. He's furious. He holds his voice low and steady but there's danger laced in his words. "Has he touched you anywhere else?"

I think of my brother's hand on my lower back, squeezing my waist, brushing my thigh. Nothing too over-the-top.

Not enough to anger Liam further.

"No," I say, shaking my head. "Nothing else like that."

Liam's dark eyes bore into mine. "Which hand does he touch you with?"

Huh? "What? Why?" Why would he ask me that?

He looms over me. "Which. Hand."

"Um," I try to think. We're all right-handed. "His right. His right hand. Why?"

"Doesn't matter. Forget him now. I never should have sent you back there. Can you forgive me?"

"Yes." I understand the choice he made. And he risked it all for me in the end, didn't he? "I forgive you."

Liam pulls me to him, placing a kiss on my forehead. The kiss is soft and sweet, a contrast to his obvious fury aimed at my brother. The kiss makes me feel warm and safe and protected.

"This is our day," he says. "Let's enjoy it." He takes my arm in his, leading me from the room.

We stand at the pink threshold of the B-Hive, looking over the outdoor wedding area they've set up for us on the main lawn. I have no family or friends to sit on the bride's side, so of course, tears prick at my eyelids to find the dozens of white chairs filled with Beauties. The Brothers sit on the groom's side, looking so handsome in their suits and tuxes.

There's an altar set up at the end of the aisle, decorated with peachy-pink David Austin rose blooms tied with Emeria-purple ribbons.

Nothing about the day is ordinary, from the impromptu bachelorette party to the fact that my husband is walking me down the aisle. Nerves weaken my knees and I lean into his arm, grateful for his strength as I walk.

Violinists in long black gowns play as we make our way. A priest waits for us, a black leather Bible in his hands. I'm not sure what I feel. Excitement, happiness, anxiousness for a future when I have no idea what to expect.

The priest begins, speaking of friends and family and love and loyalty. He continues with a blessing. "May God be with you and bless you. May you see your children's children. May you be poor in misfortune, rich in blessings. May you know nothing but happiness. From this day forward."

His voice is soothing, but I still feel drawn tight like leather over a drum. However, I decide that even though I feel these things, this uncertainty, these nerves, when I say my vows, I'll say them with my voice clear and proud.

I'm taking up my crown. I'm taking my rightful place in this crazy mafia life I was born into. I'm going to show Tess, show Liam, show my brothers, my father, everyone that I am strong and I can reign as his mafia queen—

What's that sound?

The tiniest yipping noise distracts me from the priest's words. No one hears it yet but me. I turn away from the priest, looking over my shoulder toward the sound. There—at the edge of the grass just in front of the B-Hive...

The tiniest of puppies. Just a little white bundle of fur, making its way toward me.

"Liam," I whisper. "Do you see that?"

He looks past me.

"Oh. Shit." He runs his hand over the back of his neck. "He was a wedding gift. Meant for after the ceremony. Somehow, he got out."

I turn back to Liam, in shock. "He's... for me?"

"Yes. I know how much you love things with fur and fleas, and I didn't know what else to get you so..."

I stare at my groom, then back at the little puppy making its way over the grass, unsure of what to do. It would be ridiculous, childish, unforgivable to leave your groom alone at the altar on your wedding day to chase after a ball of fluff.

But...

The puppy.

I look to Liam.

"Go on. I can wait." He dismisses me with a half-grin and a wave of his hand.

"Thank you!" I take off, glad the Beauties spared me the heels and let me get away with ivory ballet slippers for the day. I dash across the lawn, scooping up the soft little bundle in my arms. "Oh my! Hello there!"

A pink tongue darts out of a fluffy face, licking my cheek. The puppy wears a red ribbon for a collar, a tiny silver heart hanging from his neck. "Let's see."

I take the charm between my fingers, reading the inscription. *Little Pet.* "Funny. That's what Liam used to call me."

I run back to the altar, the puppy in my arms. The crowd whistles and cheers, seeing me return with my little puppy. I stretch up on tiptoe, planting a kiss on Liam's cheek. "Thank you."

"Of course."

"Why the name?" I ask, scratching Little Pet behind his ears.

"Because you're no little pet. You're my little queen. Telling you about Emily, it was like a weight was lifted from my shoulders. I'm ready to try..."

Emotions well in my chest, seeing him like this. It's the most exposed Liam's been around other people. I love that it's because of me.

"We both made confessions," I say. "I've never told anyone but you about Antonio. I guess that's what marriage is about. Letting someone in, being someone to help the other through those things."

There's a clearing of a throat. I look up at the priest.

"Ah. Are we ready to get on with this wedding?" The priest eyes me. "Or would you two like a few minutes?"

Liam nods to the priest. "We're ready."

The priest looks at the puppy. "Shall we get someone else to hold him?"

I look at Liam.

"No," Liam says. "Thank you. We're fine like this."

I hold the puppy to my chest. He curls into a little ball, nuzzling against me. "I'm ready." I hold my puppy to me with one hand, giving the other to Liam.

"In the name of God, I take you, Emilia, to be my wife, to have and to hold from this day forward, for better, for worse, for richer, for poorer, in sickness and in health, to love and to cherish, until parted by death." His voice dips. "This is my solemn vow."

I repeat the words to him. "In the name of God, I take you, Liam, to be my husband, to have and to hold from this day forward, for better, for worse, for richer, for poorer, in sickness and in health, to love and to cherish, until parted by death. This is my solemn vow."

I say the words, and I mean them. Every single one. I'm loyal, perhaps to a fault at times, but now I'll be loyal to the right person.

It's time to exchange rings.

"I'll have to give you your engagement ring and your wedding band together." Liam slips onto my finger a platinum diamond-crusted wedding band soldered to a matching band with a massive princess-cut diamond nestled in its center prongs.

"God. It's gorgeous. Thank you."

I realize I have nothing for him. Charlie saves the day, slipping a platinum wedding band in my hand. I slip it on his finger. A perfect fit.

The priest looks out over the family. "I now pronounce you Mr. and Mrs. Bachman. Liam, you may kiss your bride."

Puppy between us, Liam moves in, sliding his hands along my cheeks, bringing his lips to meet mine.

We have brunch, passing around Little Pet for cuddles as he sleeps. I sit beside my husband, sipping on champagne, taking bites of fresh melon. Tess and Rockland come to congratulate us.

We stand from our chairs. Rockland gives me the same cool kiss on my cheek. It feels like what I imagine a father's kiss might.

"You're a Beauty. Inside and out," he says. "A beautiful bride. Liam is a lucky man."

"Thank you." I will the blush to stop rising in my cheeks, but it never works.

Rockland and Liam talk, and Tess pulls me aside.

"Congratulations, sweetheart. You do make a beautiful bride." She gestures at the long tables, covered in white linen cloth and plates of fresh food. "But this? This is nothing. Forgive us, we only had a few hours. When the real thing comes, it's going to shock you."

She gives me a secret little smile.

"What do you mean?" I ask. "Like, when we have the Bachman-only ceremony?"

"Yes." She nods, putting a cool hand on my forearm. "We had to do this because of the timing, get the legal marriage underway, the paperwork filed, appease the families you've upset, but to us, the real wedding is the one we throw. And it's going to be gorgeous."

Butterflies tickle my stomach at the idea of yet another party, though I can't imagine one more lavish than this. "I can't wait."

"See you in New York." She gives me a squeeze. I receive a parting cheek kiss from Rockland, then he offers Tess his arm, and the incredibly gorgeous and perfect-looking couple glide off to speak with other guests.

We take our seats. Liam slides his arm around my shoulders, the weight of it like a blanket wrapped around me. I'm suddenly so very tired. The early morning, the party, the nerves at the wedding. I'm just bone-tired. I love it here. I love the beach and the Beauties. I'm literally in paradise.

So I can't believe I'm asking this. But I am. "It's beautiful here, but do you think..." My words trail off. We've only been married all of what? An hour or two? How can I tell him I just want to change into my leggings and sweatshirt, curl up on the big leather seat of the jet with Little Pet on my lap, snuggle in beside him and go back to his place?

He wraps an arm around my lower back, pulling me into him. He kisses my cheek. "Let's go home."

Home. Back to The Villa. Where I belong.

I nestle against him, my hand against his chest, relieved by his words. I think of the pretty lake and the mountains and the pool

I've not yet sat beside. More importantly, the orange tabby I need to somehow bring inside and the little monkey I still need to tame.

I think of Marta and her soft voice and her good cooking. I think of sweet, funny Charlie who'll be traveling back with us. I think of his brothers who, despite their unruliness, treat me with respect and kindness.

"Yes," I say. "Let's go. Home."

18

L *iam*

"THERE'S NO FUCKING WAY THAT DOG IS SLEEPING IN THIS BED." I stare at the white ball of fur that's invaded my life. "Why is Little Pet curled up at the foot of our bed like he owns the place? There is one master of this castle and that's me."

She pats the dog on the head. "Oh, we know who's in charge around here."

Infuriating.

"Do you need a reminder?" I go to her, grabbing her around the waist and pin her to the bed.

She giggles, swatting at my shoulder. Her laughter dissolves as I slide my hand over her breast, hooking my fingers around her neck.

I tap my fingers along her skin, lashing her earlobe with the tip of my tongue. "I'm happy to show you."

Her pretty little dog leaps up, yipping and turning circles on the duvet.

I groan, dropping my head to her chest. "Fuck me for ever getting you that dog."

"How 'bout you fuck me, and we keep the dog. I love him." She laughs.

I push the dog to the side, kissing her lips. "And me?"

"I like you pretty well too." She kisses me back and I know she likes me more than just pretty well. Her tongue slips in my mouth, caressing mine. She's hungry for me.

I need the dog gone.

He's settled back down on the covers, his eyes trained on me. "He's watching us. It's creepy."

"No. It's fine. Kiss me." She wraps her arms around my neck.

"It's not. It's really not."

She takes a deep breath, sighing at my unwillingness to accept the dog being a voyeur to our sex life. Her breasts rise against my chest as she breathes. I have to have her.

Now.

"You haven't been to the pool yet. Have you?" I ask.

Before she can answer, I scoop her up in my arms. She laughs, her hold around my neck tightening. I carry her from the room, kicking the door shut behind me.

Goodnight, Little Pet.

Time for me to taste my little queen.

I carry her down to the pool, flipping the ground lights on that illuminate the path. The evening is clear and cool, stars dotting a midnight sky. I keep the pool heated and steam rises from the lit-up blue-green water, inviting us in.

"No bathing suits? What if someone sees us?" she asks.

"No one will come. If the lights for the path are on at night, it's our signal to one another. Stay away."

I set her down on her bare feet on the stone patio. She wears cotton pajama shorts and a tank.

Nothing else.

"My God, you're gorgeous. How is it the less you do, the prettier you are?" I grab at the hem of her tank, lifting it up over her smooth belly. "Let's see just how beautiful you are. Lift your arms, wife."

When I say wife, her cheeks go all pink. She loves it when I call her wife. She raises her arms in the air, her breasts, her nipples straining against the thin material.

I want to see more. I tug the shirt from her arms, tossing it to the ground.

And I just stare.

She really is the most beautiful thing I've ever seen.

And she's all mine.

Why did I resist this marriage thing for so long?

I stare down at the flimsy cotton shorts knowing she wears no panties. "I want to taste my little wifey. I want to see how sweet she is."

She watches as I drag my shirt up over my back. I drop it on the ground by the edge of the pool. I'll be needing it. I step out of my sweatpants and underwear, leaving them with the shirt.

I turn, leaving her standing alone on the stone, bare-breasted, and I jump down into the pool. I slice under the water.

When I rise, her eyes are on me. I push my wet hair back from my eyes. "Bring my shirt and come over here."

"Where? Into the water?" She's shy now, covering her breasts with her crossed arms. She steps around the pool toward me, but her movements are slow.

"No." I pat the ground right in front of me. "Here."

She's made it over to me, standing above me. The lights from the pool illuminate her face, water reflecting dancing lines across her skin. She's so beautiful, it makes me ache. I take my shirt, folding it into a square and putting it down at her feet.

My voice is thick and I hold it steady. "Take off your shorts."

I watch as she pushes the thin fabric over her hips. They drop around her ankles. She gives them a little kick.

And there she is. Just her. Naked and natural. I love her in the gowns, the expensive jewelry, the makeup, her hair done up in all sorts of elaborate ways.

But this... this is mine.

Just pure, sweet Emilia.

"You're perfect. You know that?"

"I don't know about that." She crouches down, trying to maintain some shred of modesty as she sits by the pool. She gives a sigh as her slender legs dip into the warm water. "This water is perfect. I've always thought it would be so nice to have a pool."

"Everything I have is yours." I circle an ankle with my fingers, spreading her legs to move between them.

She gazes out over the lake, the mountains, now blue and black in the night. "It's so beautiful here. So peaceful."

"The Villa is your home now. And I promise to keep it as peaceful as I can." Now, with her here, the idea of bringing work inside these walls pains me. "We're no longer a bachelor pad. We have precious cargo."

"Thank you." She leans forward, putting her hands on my cheeks. She kisses me. The moment her lips touch mine, a fire sets in my belly.

Her smooth thighs press against either side of my torso as she kisses me. When she pulls away, I glance down at her pretty sex, hungry for a taste. I smooth my hands up her thighs, grabbing her around her hips. I pull her to the very edge of the pool, my T-shirt protecting her skin from the concrete.

"Your lips are so sweet. Now I want to taste that pretty little pussy. Wife."

"You talk so dirty," she reprimands with a *tsk tsk* sound, then gives a naughty grin. "I love it."

I move between her thighs, parting her soft skin with my fingers. I love seeing the hidden parts of her sex, knowing I'm the only man on this Earth who's ever laid eyes on this paradise.

All mine.

I slide my tongue up the center of her sex, making circles around her clit. Her hands go to my shoulders as she breathes out my name. "Oh, Liam."

My name sounds so sweet on her lips. It... does things to me. Makes me feel things I thought I'd buried away forever. As I lick and kiss her and listen to her soft breaths and moans, my name slips out again.

"Liam... God. Liam."

The sound makes a fierce desire to protect her rise in my chest. I must keep her safe. I pull away, saying, "There's one thing that will help me keep things peaceful here. Make me one promise."

Hearing the serious tone in my voice, she opens her eyes, finding mine. "What?"

"Never, ever leave this property without telling me first. I won't keep you prisoner here, but I won't let you go out there alone. I have beautiful cars and armed men you can have your pick of to escort you if you ever need to go without me. But never go alone."

But she's too heady from her pleasure to focus. "Oh my God, can you stop talking? I'm dying here."

"Rude, naughty girl." I punish her with a nip of my teeth on her inner thigh. I stand back up, squeezing her legs in my hands, my gaze burning into hers.

This is too important to not get an answer from her. "Promise me." I need to hear the words.

"Okay, I promise! I promise. But honestly, why would I ever want to leave?"

Her answer satisfies me and finally, I dive back down, my full mouth on her glorious pussy, devouring her until she comes, once, twice, a third time, her body curling around me, her fingers tearing at my hair, her lips whisper-shouting my name.

Liam. Liam. Liam.

I pull away, dragging my mouth along her inner thigh. I stand, slipping my hands into her hair. "Taste how sweet you are."

"I don't know." She tries to pull away from my kiss, but I bring her in, kissing her hard, swiping my tongue along hers so she can taste her sex. I love how shy, how virginal, how inexperienced she is, but she balances it with heat and desire, now leaning into my kiss, stroking her tongue against mine.

I slide my hands under her arms, pulling her down onto me and into the pool. I hold her body against mine in the water, kissing her.

A rustling sound parts our kiss.

She slides into the water and presses into me, hiding her breasts against my chest as she looks around. "I thought you said no one would come out here?"

"They won't. It's probably just your damn cat."

"Oh," she smiles, looking over my shoulder. "There."

"What?" I turn to look behind me.

The damn monkey of Po's is sitting on my sweatpants, staring at us.

"Aww. Isn't he so cute? Marta's making banana bread tomorrow morning. I'm going to see if he will come to me."

"No," I say, "you will not. That thing could have fleas or rabies or—"

"Shh..." she says. "Kiss me."

I want to kiss her, but I can't with that damn monkey staring at me.

I stare him down. "I swear to God I will kill every pet on this godforsaken property if they do not let me fuck my wife."

"Liam! Don't say that."

My shouts make the monkey turn, disappearing back into the bushes. Good riddance.

I swim-walk her over to the edge, lifting her and sitting her back down on my shirt. "Wait here. I'll get towels. We're going back in the house."

"But why? It's so nice out here." She tilts her head back, looking at the stars. "I love the feel of the night air."

"Because. The damn cat will probably be next. I don't want any interruptions when I make love to my wife."

My words hang in the air between us. Where did that come from? Make love?

She flushes, looking away. "Okay. I'll wait here."

I take a breather, leaving the pool to go to the stocked cabinet by the outdoor showers to grab a stack of towels. After a quick rinse under the warm water, I tie one around my waist, my erection fully gone from the sight of that damn monkey, and dry my hair with the other.

She's only gotten wet from the waist down, so I bring a towel to dry her with.

She's waiting by the pool, right where I left her, dragging her toes lazily in the water.

Forget the dog. Forget the monkey. Forget the cat.

I'm having her.

Now.

Instead of drying her, I spread the towel in the soft grass, fold my legs in and sit beside it. "Come here," I call to her.

With the grace of a dancer, she stands, coming to me. "I thought we were going in."

"Change of plans. You were loving the night air. And I want you. Now."

She lies down on the towel, her golden hair a halo as it spreads out behind her. She looks delicious, a dish to be devoured. Her gaze lingers on my tattoo, her fingers lazily tracing the design. I capture her hand in mine and dive between her thighs again, drawing another orgasm from her beautiful body. Her knees tremble as they press against me, her fingers leaving mine, raking through my drying hair.

Her words come breathy and high-pitched. "I can't take anymore."

"Take it, babygirl." And I dive back down, licking and sucking her. I thrust two fingers into her at once, crooking my fingers, stroking her velvety sex.

She comes again, pulling the hair from my scalp. "Oh my... God!"

I rise, wiping my mouth on the back of my hand. I take her in, flushed face, shining eyes, her breasts rising and falling with heavy breaths. I grab her hips, flipping her over onto her knees.

She gives a throaty, lusty laugh, tossing her head and her hair over her shoulder to flash me a sexy look.

Fuck.

A growl escapes me as I plunge my cock into her sweet, slippery sex. "God, you're so tight, so wet for me. You feel so good."

I pull back, running a hand down her spine, caressing her back, my other hand tugging at her hips, bringing her ass up higher. She lays her head down on her arms on the lawn, a deep moan leaving her as I thrust into her again.

The beginnings of ecstasy quake through me, tightening my balls, blood rushing through my core. I move in and out of her, smoothing my hand down her back, raking my fingers over her smooth skin. She's so beautiful like this, her back, her curves.

Suddenly, a deep need to see her face tears through me. "I need to see you." I pull out of her, turning her over once more.

I push her hair back from her face, the look of trust, of desire so deep in her eyes I find myself kissing her so hard my lips bruise. I slide a hand beneath her head, cradling her as I kiss her. I push inside her. Her legs wrap around my waist, her arms, around my neck.

It feels like we are... one.

Being inside her like this, our bodies tangled, our mouths joined tight, it's the freest I've felt.

Ever.

Free like I'm flying, like I'm weightless, like nothing matters in this world. At the same time, tied down tight, bound to her, a fear of anything ever hurting her creeps into my chest.

This time, I face the fear head-on.

I won't run.

She's worth the risk.

The only woman who could tame me.

When I come, it's her name on my lips. "Emilia."

From now on, it will always be hers.

19

E *milia*

HOW IS IT THAT I'M FALLING FOR HIM?

I've always been loyal. Maybe it was making that vow that allowed me to open my heart, my mind, to the idea of not just marrying him, but one day...

Falling in love with him.

Last night, by the lake. That wasn't fucking. Well, there was some fucking, at the beginning, but by the end, it was...

Lovemaking.

I don't want any interruptions when I'm making love to my wife. That's what he said. Making love.

I kneel by the bushes, holding a square of Marta's homemade banana bread still warm from the oven, dressed in my uniform of workout clothes: black leggings, white tank, and a fitted black running jacket zipped up to the collar, only now the material is buttery smooth against my skin, the designer label a silver tag over my breast.

Today, I picked the teal and blue Nike running shoes from the endless supply of options that line the shelves of the closet I now own in Liam's suite. A closet the same size as my bedroom at my father's house. Drawers built into the walls are filled with T-shirts and tanks made from organic cotton, all folded into neat squares.

Liam and I have our own bathrooms with sinks and a toilet room, a massive shower with two heads and a rain shower in the middle.

We've yet to shower alone.

"Come here, little *scimmia*." I know he's in the bushes, I hear him moving around in the leaves. I hold the bread out. Was this a good choice? Should I have brought him something else? "Come, come."

My patience is rewarded. He pokes his little tan face out from the green leaves. "There you are."

He takes the bread from my hand with his nimble fingers. He nibbles at the corner, eyeing me curiously. I left Little Pet locked inside, fearful he would chase the monkey if I got this close.

Footsteps slap the stone behind us, sending my monkey back into the bushes.

"Hey you. You scared my friend away." I know it's him before I even turn my head. I know the sound of his footsteps. I can sense his presence the moment just before he walks into a room.

"That fleabag? Good riddance." But his tone is soft.

He's already let Po capture the cat and take him to the vet for me. He's in Marta's kitchen right now, getting fat on the scraps she's feeding him.

I stand, brushing breadcrumbs and grass from my clothing.

"Come here." He wraps his arms around me, pulling me in for a kiss.

I take in his dark eyes, his handsome face.

What's this?

I stroke his cheek; there's something red just under his jawline. I scratch it with my finger and it flakes off, trapped under my pink manicured nail. A bit of dried blood?

"What happened?" I ask.

"What?" He looks down at my hand. "That?"

His fingers go to his jawline. "Probably just cut myself shaving."

But there's another dot on the white collar of his business shirt. He's so careful, I'm surprised he'd overlook it. "There's more. Here." I finger the starched material.

"I guess I'm becoming careless. Someone has me distracted lately."

I drag my arms around his neck, leaning up on tiptoe for a kiss. "And who would that be?"

"My little wife. My queen." He tugs at the end of my ponytail. He kisses me.

I've never felt this happy before. It scares me. I feel like it could slip through my fingers at any moment.

His kiss deepens.

The happiness grows.

He gives my ass a smack, pulling away from me. "Come on. We've got to go."

"I was going to go for a run. You have other plans for me?"

He takes my hand, leading me toward the house. "Yes. Charlie's meeting us."

"Oh. Why's that?"

"She decorated this house. Did a beautiful job, so I'm told by the women in my life—"

"You mean Charlie and Marta?" I laugh.

"Yes." He tugs my hand, catching my eye. "But I want the house to feel like you."

"I love the decorating she's done," I say. "We don't have to change a thing."

He flashes a secret smile. "You might have a different opinion when you see what I have in mind."

"Okay." Butterflies tickle at my tummy, my heart pattering with excitement as we step into the house.

He walks me to a wing deeper on the first floor. There are so many rooms, I've not been in all of them yet. We reach a closed door, painted white, its knob crystal. He opens the door. It's an empty room, its walls painted a bright white. The windows overlook the lake. It's a blank slate.

"This room we left. We weren't sure what to do with it at the time. It's all yours for anything you want. I was thinking maybe a workout room if you don't want to keep using the gym with the guys," he says.

My footsteps echo as I step into the room. Gym. That's an understatement for what he has at this house. It's a state-of-the-art training facility with every type of equipment you could want. Besides, I like hearing the friendly banter of the men as they work out, spotting one another on the weights while I run on the treadmill.

Three tall rectangular windows stand at one end of the room, forming a little nook. The perfect place for a reading bench or a built-in window seat. The kind of room every lover of books dreams of owning.

"No." I shake my head. "I like the gym. But I know just what this room should be. A library."

"It's all yours. Anything you want," he says.

Anything I want...

I'm not used to hearing those words.

I'm not used to thinking about what would make me happy.

I guess it's time to start.

"There is one thing you could do for me," I say. "Please."

"Anything."

"My mother's books. They're at my father's house, in the library there. The boys don't read them. They don't care for reading." And they won't care for my books. "I'd love to have shelves built along the walls. It would mean the world to me if her books were on those shelves."

"You'll have them by the end of the day." He kisses the top of my head. "Charlie will be here soon. I've got some things to attend to, including getting your books. I'll leave you to it."

Charlie comes, her hair in curls, her arms loaded with stacks of leather-bound books. We go through choosing paint colors for the walls, a deep hunter green like the library at the Parish, and wood for the shelving, a honey-colored teak, dark brown natural streaks running through it. The lighting will be black metal, the bulbs the kind that show the filament, a pretty little orange glow.

Charlie helps me choose an upholstery fabric for the cushions she'll have made for the window seat we'll design.

We have lunch in the dining room. Marta brings us slices of pineapple and watermelon, a quinoa salad rich with feta and olive oil, and thick slices of warm bread, its crust flaking when you bite into it.

I go for my run. Liam's had a pebbled path installed all the way around the property, within its stone walls where I'm safe. It circles through the garden, the blooms scenting my run. After a shower, I snuggle down in the bed with Little Pet curled up by my side and a book from one of the shelves in the room I first stayed in.

Marta surprises me with an afternoon coffee in bed, the rich liquid laced with sugar and cream.

Later that day the books come, packed neatly in crates. Mattia delivers them. I meet him on the stone entryway porch.

Next to the crates is a bin with a lid. I open it to see what's inside. "What's this?"

Oh my God—bless the man. He found the books under my bed and packed them in the bin. In this house, those books could proudly line the shelves of my library. I close the lid.

He laughs. "I knew you'd want *all* of your books. You thought the ones under your bed were a secret, but I've seen you on your hands and knees before, pulling out books. When I was packing up, I went to your room and found them."

"Thanks," I say with a smile.

When I ask about the house, and our father, he hesitates, then says, "Everything is good. Pretty much the same."

I don't want to, but I need to ask. "And Antonio?"

Mattia won't meet my eye. "Antonio... well, he's had a change of heart. He's... different now."

"Different, how?"

"Nothing." He shrugs. "It's nothing. He realizes he was a shit to you."

"Really?"

"Yeah. We all do. We just... we miss you. That's all. And I miss you kicking my ass at the gym."

I laugh, tears almost coming to my eyes. His words surprise me. The last thing I thought was that they'd miss me, that Antonio would ever feel anything but hatred toward me.

"I'll come see you all for dinner sometime."

He shakes his head. "I don't think your husband would like that."

"Well, I'm not a prisoner here." I know Liam said I wasn't a prisoner here, that I can go anywhere if I have him or an escort, but we both knew when he said it that left unspoken was that going home was off the table.

My brother is thinking the same thing. "No. Don't come home. It's not a good idea. Just stay here. Look around. Why would you ever want to come back to our shithole?" He gives a half laugh.

"But you have money now, right? From Liam? You can fix it up." I think of the beauty the house held when my mother lived there. "Maybe I can help you."

Mattia gazes up at the crystal chandelier hanging over my head. "Don't bother, Em. Just enjoy what you have here."

I must ask. "Are you? Fixing up the house at all?"

"Dad thinks he's got better things to do with the money." He tries to smile. "Take care of yourself. I heard the gym here is amazing."

"Maybe you can come sometime."

He shoots me a *don't be dumb* look. "Bye, Em."

"Goodbye, Mattia. Thank you for the books."

I close the door. I leave the books. The men will bring them into the library for me. I've been told not to lift a finger.

For dinner, Liam surprises me with a boat ride on the lake. Po and Cannon and Charlie join us. Liam looks sexy driving a boat, his shirt off, dark sunglasses on his handsome face. He drives fast, the air whipping my hair around my face, the wake behind us white and foaming. He anchors the boat in the middle of the lake and we dive off the side, swimming and splashing in the water like kids.

Cannon swims up to me, pushing his dark hair out of his eyes. It's the same color as Liam's but with curls instead of waves. One lock falls over his aquamarine eyes, the color stunning like the water of the lake.

He gives a devil's grin. His voice is low, sultry. He cocks a dark brow at me, speaking slowly. "You've got to come to my club some time, *pupino.* I think you and your husband would love to have a session."

Is this what Charlie means when she says Cannon is the "smoothest" of all the brothers? My vanilla—only not been a virgin for about a minute—is surely showing in the heat that rises in my cheeks. "I... um..."

He glides through the water, circling me like a shark. The smile on his face tells me he's loving this, making the little bride blush. His eyes, more blue than green upon further inspection, give a sexy flash. "Tell me. Have you ever had eyes on you when you—"

"Cannon!" My husband's voice roars from the bow of the boat.

Oh shit. Little brother is in big trouble. I look up at Liam, relieved to find a grin on his face. Cannon will live to see another day.

Liam bellows, "Leave her alone, you son of a bitch, or I'm coming down there to drown you."

Cannon laughs, a deep, throaty sound that must drive single women mad with lust. "Do your best, old man!" He splashes water up toward Liam.

Liam does a perfect dive, slicing into the water, ripples running in his wake.

I giggle as Liam pops up out of the water behind Cannon, taking him in a headlock. Liam growls at his brother, "What have I told you about growing a filter? Just because you think your dirty thoughts doesn't mean you can say them to my wife." He dunks Cannon under, pulling him back up. "I should kill you for even thinking them."

Cannon grabs at Liam's forearm, sputtering and laughing. "Brother! Relax. I'm just looking out for the business. You're always telling me to choose my investments wisely. And you and your wife would bring quite a crowd."

"My wife is not stepping foot inside your club." Liam dunks his brother under the water. Cannon fights back, the two of them wrestling in the water, hurling good-natured insults at one another. I've never seen Liam so playful before.

I love it.

When Cannon swims away, Liam takes me in his arms, gliding me through the water. His lips tickle my ear. "I hope you know he's joking. We brothers live by our own code. Never, ever touch another man's woman. They may flirt, but it's all innocent."

"And the club?" I ask, running my toes over the tops of his feet beneath the water.

Jealousy flashes in his gaze briefly. "Never. Men would be lined up for blocks to see you play, but you, my little queen, you are for my eyes only. "The only way you'll be playing at the club is with me in one of the private rooms we reserve for the family. Never in public."

"Never say never," I tease. My joke earns me a hard squeeze of my ass and a biting kiss on the back of my neck.

Heaven never felt so close.

When our muscles ache from swimming, the men sit on the leather boat seats, discussing opening new clubs. One day I'll take an interest, showing Liam that I too can help with the family business. I want to pull my weight, but for today, I'll worship the sun. Charlie and I lay side by side on a thick quilt spread over the bow, tanning in the warm air of the late afternoon.

We dine from a basket Marta prepared. Cheese and fruit and bread, delicate slices of meat, chilled champagne, sparkling flavored waters.

Liam feeds me bites of chocolate truffles while we watch the sun set over the horizon, the sky a burst of orange and pink and red.

When we get home, we shower together. He washes my hair, rubbing his sudsy hands all over my body. When he pushes me up against the warm tile wall and takes me again, it feels less like fucking and more like lovemaking. He kisses a trail down my neck, his mouth finding my breast. He sucks at my nipple, nipping it between his teeth. He scoops me up under my ass, bringing my legs around his waist and as my back presses into the wall, I think about that first time in my room, when he snuck onto my balcony.

He murmurs in my ear, "Emilia. I care about you... so much."

My sex tightens around him as I hold him closer, locking my legs around his waist. We move together, like we were made for one another, like we're one body, not two. He moves in me hard and fast, keeping pace with my racing heart, the whoosh of it loud in my ears. Joy fills my chest as intense gratification spills through my body, my sex clenching and pulsing, my breasts heaving. He chases me down, in and out, over and over till he reaches his peak. His cock jerks inside me, pulsing. It fills me with his cum, spilling out, flowing down my thighs.

Afterward, he washes himself from me. I almost wish I didn't have this IUD. We'd make incredibly cute babies together.

I snuggle down into the fluffy white comforter, Little Pet curled between us. Liam doesn't even complain, just pats the dog on the head. "Little shit."

There's a meow at the door.

I sit up, keeping a hand on the puppy's collar to keep him from going after the cat. "Oh look, it's Mr. Patches."

"No way. No fucking way."

A moment later, there's a cat curled at my dear husband's feet.

"His fur is growing in nicely since he's been staying in the house, don't you think?" I say.

"Fuck my life," Liam says, throwing an arm over his eyes.

But the smile on his face reaches all the way down to my toes.

When I wake, Liam's gone, the covers rumpled on his empty side of the bed. There's coffee waiting for me on the nightstand, sitting on one of the electronic warming pads they keep all over the house. These men love their coffee.

With the push of a button, the blinds raise, showing me the morning sunlight sparkling over the water. I sit, petting my dog, enjoying the view as I sip my coffee. I take my time getting ready for my day. Who knows what it will bring? Charlie and I are lifting weights together this afternoon. I'll run after that. I go casual, sneakers and jeans, a soft, long-sleeved tee, figuring I can skip the workout clothes for once.

I make my way to the first floor, my hand slowly slipping down the polished railing. I feel like a queen descending the stairs of my castle. Marta waits for me in the kitchen with freshly squeezed orange juice and muffins she must have baked this morning.

"Sit, sit." She pulls out my chair.

I take a bite of the muffin, still warm, berries bursting in my mouth. "Marta, these are amazing. Will you teach me how to bake one day?"

She laughs, waving a hand in the air. "You have no need for that. You're the lady of the house. No work for you."

"Okay, Marta." I wash down the muffin with juice, wondering if she means it or just doesn't want anyone on her turf. The kitchen is Marta's territory. I've heard she only lets staff in to pick up the food to deliver to other rooms.

She goes to the sink, busying herself with clean up. "So, what are you getting into today?"

"A little bit of this and that. I'm taking Little Pet for a walk in the garden. I'm going to try to coax Po's monkey out again."

"No luck with my banana bread?"

"Yes! He loved it, but then Liam came and scared him away." I expect her to laugh but my words make a flash of tension dance over her face. It's gone as quickly as it came, but I saw it there. "Everything alright, Marta?"

She nods. "Of course, of course!"

"Okay."

"Did you see your brother Antonio yesterday when your family delivered the books?" she asks.

"No. It was Mattia that came. Why?"

"Nothing. No reason." She scrubs at the bottom of her big soup pot. "It's just that... I heard your oldest brother, he recently... lost a lot of weight. Kind of quickly. Overnight, really. I was wondering how he was doing."

"Antonio?" Mattia didn't mention any illness. The thought of my brother sick worries me. Even if he was a total ass to me the past few years. Mattia's words ring in my mind, the idea that Antonio has turned over a new leaf, that he regrets the way he treated me. "I should go see him."

Marta scrubs her pot harder. "I don't think that's a good idea. You shouldn't go home now. I just—I don't even know why I told you. Stay here. I'll ask about him and get back to you."

"Alright, I will. Thank you." My loyalties lie with the Bachmans now, but the thought of Antonio being sick stays with me. I need to go home, just to check on him. He's still my brother. I won't tell Marta. She'll only worry about me.

And as far as Liam goes? I promised him I wouldn't leave the property without telling him. So, I will tell him.

When I'm back, safe and sound.

There's no reason to stress Mr. Grumpy out. I'll just grab the horse, pop down to the house, check on Antonio, and pop back.

I walk to the stables, hoping the horse I rode home on once made it back that night I sent him home alone and is now here. If he is, I'll call him...

Journey.

And I'll call the monkey Banana Bread. Little Pet, Patches, Banana Bread, and Journey. One big, happy family.

The pale gray horse is waiting just like last time. It takes a little while to get him ready; I'm going with the saddle this time. Then, we're off.

I nudge Journey's side softly with my foot. "We'll be back soon."

We take off into the woods.

20

E *milia*

THE PLACE LOOKS... OKAY. NOT MUCH MONEY'S BEEN INVESTED YET, but the grass has been cut and one of my brothers, Cass, is gathering brush, burning it in a bonfire in a small clearing. The shutter's been fixed.

I give a wave, and to my delight, he waves back.

I pat the horse. "You wait right here for me. Okay? I'll be back." I loop the reins loosely over the wooden post at the front steps of the house. I grab a hose, filling an old, empty ceramic flowerpot with clean water for Journey.

I go up the steps to the front door. My hand rests on the cold metal doorknob. I never know what I'll find inside.

"Hello?" I call out to the empty foyer. The curtains, instead of being replaced, have been removed completely, sunlight cascading over the dark wood floors.

"In here."

I go to the dining room.

Silas sits at the table, working. He glances up at me, his gray eyes brightening. "Emilia, what are you doing here?"

There are thick rectangular packages on the dining room table, first wrapped in a layer of brown paper, then plastic. There must be a hundred of them neatly stacked there. I've seen packages like this before. The Meralos, down at the dock. One of the brothers dropped a cooler onto the dock and one of the packages fell out. His brother hit him, whispering angrily about how stupid his mistake was.

The Meralos sell cocaine. Bachman's don't touch the stuff. This is going to be a problem.

No. No way. Icy tendrils creep up my spine. "Are those... drugs?"

"Good to see you, sis." He ignores my question, going back to his stacking. "It's our new business. Our investment. Thank you, by the way, for the starter fee. We'll multiply your dowry by ten before the end of the year."

"What's in those packages?"

He flashes me a grin. "You don't need to know, pretty girl. Just go back to your castle. Leave the peasants to do the dirty work."

He grabs a big, black duffle bag from a chair, carefully laying packages inside.

"Could you not have found a different business to invest in?" I ask.

"Not one this profitable." His voice softens a touch. Maybe he did miss me. "Don't worry yourself, Emilia. We're fine."

There's a knock on the doorframe. Antonio hovers in the doorway. The sight of my older brother makes my stomach flip with anxiety.

"Leave us, Silas?" he says.

"Sure." Silas puts the bag back down on the chair. He gives me a look as he leaves. "Take care. Okay?"

"Yeah, sure." I nod, unused to these small acts of kindness from my brothers. "You too."

Antonio doesn't enter the room. He stays by the open threshold, half hidden by the wall. "How've you been?"

His green eyes are soft and for a moment I'm transported back in time to when we were children in my mother's garden, Antonio chasing me, the two of us laughing.

"Well," I say. "And you?"

"I want to say something to you. I'm sorry. I was an ass. I don't want to blame it on Mom dying, or Dad being harsh. It was all me. I'm mean, I've got a streak of anger inside me I can't seem to control and sometimes..." He looks away, his voice breaking. "Sometimes you just remind me so damn much of her. And it hurts. And... it made me want to hurt you."

"What?" His words settle around me and I try to absorb them, make sense of them.

He doesn't hate me?

He hates that I remind him of Mom.

"Do I really?" I ask. "Have her in me?"

He nods. "Every bit. You're strong like her and calm like her. And beautiful. And I'm sorry."

"Thanks." I brush back the tears welling up in my eyes. "Thank you, for that."

He steps clear of the doorway. Something silver by his right hand catches my eyes. What is that? What the...

"Antonio." I step toward him, getting a better look. "Is that a hook, in your hand?"

He holds up his right hand. I gasp. He's not holding anything in his hand. There is no hand.

The hook *is* his hand.

I rush to him, all bad memories erased by the sight of his hand. "What happened? Oh my God, what happened to you?"

"It was an accident," he says. "I got it mangled in some equipment. The doctor couldn't save it."

White heat flashes over my skin. I think I'm going to be sick. "I'm so sorry. Are you okay—"

But I let the stupid question drop. Of course he's not.

To my surprise, his eyes rise to meet mine. "I am, actually. The... accident, helped me see things with a new perspective. I don't know. It's fine. It made me see how I mistreated you." His green eyes grow cold, dark. "And gave me a new determination about my place in this world."

I don't know what to do, so I just stand there, trying not to stare at the silver cap and hook above his wrist.

"Go back, Emilia. Things here have changed." His eyes trail to what I assume are packages of cocaine on the table. "You can't be here anymore."

"Why not?"

He doesn't answer, just looks away.

Are the drugs the reason I can't be here, or is it something else?

"Antonio, look at me."

He won't meet my eye.

It's something else.

I look at his hand. His *right* hand.

"Wait," I say, my skin turning to ice. "This wasn't an accident. Was it? Who did this to you?"

"It doesn't matter. It's over." He shakes his head. "You need to leave. Now."

Oh my God, husband. What have you done?

LIAM

MARTA COMES TO ME RIGHT AWAY TO TELL ME EMILIA'S TAKEN OFF with the horse. "I'm sorry, sir. I slipped, telling her Antonio had... lost some weight. I only meant for her to call him, check on him, not go there. I've really messed this up." She's wringing her hands, pacing the floor.

I put a hand on her shoulder to calm her. "She was going to find out eventually. Thank you for telling me she left." I grab my keys. "I'm going to get her now."

My cell rings. I've been so busy I haven't gotten one for Emilia yet. I didn't think she'd need one. I thought she'd keep her promise and she'd always be with me or one of my men who could easily contact me.

I look down at the screen. Thank God. It's the Accardi landline.

I answer, hoping to hear her voice on the other end. "Hello?"

"Liam, its Emilia."

"Thank God. What were you thinking, taking off like that? On horseback, no less?" Now that I've heard her voice, anger rises in me. "How could you leave like that?"

"I had to check on my brother. And," she takes a deep breath, "I'm not coming home yet."

I give a dark chuckle. "That's funny."

"I'm serious, Liam. After what you did, I'll ride back to The Villa when I'm ready. I need a minute. A little space."

"You can have all the space you want." I glance around at the massive room I stand in, the twenty-foot ceilings. "It's a big house we have here."

"Space, as in I'm not coming to the house. Not right now. I'm staying at my dad's for a little while."

Hell. No.

"No, you're not," I say into the phone. "Even if I have to tie you up, drag you out of that house, throw you over my shoulder, and put you in my car, you're coming home."

"No. I need some time away." Her voice shakes. "What you did..."

I lower my tone. "What I did, I had to do."

"You had to do? Are you kidding?" She's pissed, her voice rising. "You cut my brother's hand off!"

I don't understand. Why is she mad? She should be happy to have her vengeance. "He touched you. He never should have touched you. What was I supposed to do?"

"I don't know," she huffs into the phone. "Maybe, *not* cut his hand off?"

"It had to be done."

"My brother has a... Hook. For. A. Hand. A hook!"

"That's nice. It'll come in handy in mafia life. You never know when you'll need a hook. Could be useful—"

Her voice stays cold. "You cut my brother's hand off. Off. Of his body."

The fury returns when she says the word *body*. It makes me think of her body, how her brother defiled her beautiful breasts. "He touched you with that hand. If anyone else touches you, I'll do the same."

"Liam!"

"I'll bet he's glad he didn't commit incest."

It takes a moment for my words to settle in. "Oh my God. Liam. Stop." Her tone goes sad, ripping at my heart. "Couldn't you just let it go?"

"What kind of husband, leader, would I be if I let it go?" I say. "I had to do something about it and I did."

"Do you feel better?"

"Yes. Very much so." But I don't. Not now that she's upset.

"Well, I don't! My brother is out there walking around like Captain Hook or something and all you can do is—"

"Stop." I interrupt her. Even if she's mad, she still has to face me. She broke a promise to me. "I don't want to talk about your brother anymore. I want to talk about your promise. The promise you made to me."

A hint of fear rings in her voice. "Which one?"

"To not leave without telling me."

"I had to check on my brother. I heard he wasn't well. But that's not what we're talking about." The fear turns to an icy chill as she says her next words. "What about the promise you made to me?"

"Which one?"

"To cherish me," she says. "Is cutting off the hand of my brother really cherishing me?"

"Yes," I say. "I cut off his hand because I cherish you. He had to be punished. Let it be a warning to him, to your father, to your brothers, to every man in this country that you are not to be touched."

"Yeah, I think you made that clear. What are you going to do if someone shakes my hand? Helps me out of a car? Is our town going to be littered with one-handed men?"

How can she compare what he did to a handshake?

My voice goes cold. "Antonio did *not* shake your hand."

Silence.

She sighs. "You're right. I know. He was wrong, but this just seems so..."

"Welcome to the mafia, Emilia."

Her voice grows tight. "This is exactly why I didn't want to marry. You men do stupid, stupid things. You lose your tempers, cut off body parts, kill one another, start wars. And hurt innocent people in the process."

"I won't apologize for this, Emilia," I say. "He deserved what he got. He's lucky I didn't kill him."

"Kill him! He's my brother."

"I know."

"So, what if I piss you off? Huh? What then? Are you going to do something like that to me?" She sounds close to tears.

My tone softens. "No. I would never, ever hurt you. Only those that hurt you."

"God. You... *men*. Ugh. I just can't understand you all. This isn't what I wanted for my life."

"This *is* your life. And you *are* my wife. Accept it."

"Accept, accept. I know." She heaves a sigh. "I know, Tess told me the same thing. I just, I—I need a minute."

"You can have all the minutes you want. Be as angry with me as you want. I don't care. But you're going to do it from the safety of this house. I'm coming to get you. Now."

She waits a bit, anger and disappointment hanging over the line between us. "Fine."

"Fine. Stay put. I'll be there in fifteen minutes." I hang up the phone.

I've never driven so fast in my life, taking the curves of the road practically on two wheels, leaving rubber from my tires behind.

Smoke. That's... smoke. In the air, coming from the woods, from the Accardi property. My heart lurches out of my chest, my stomach plummeting fifty feet. No. This can't be happening. Not again. All my fears... everything I've worried over—I stop my torrent of thoughts, needing my head clear.

Smoke does not always mean death.

I must remember that.

I take a deep breath. I turn down the drive. An Accardi brother is burning brush in a clearing by their gothic mansion. The source of the smoke. I take a deep breath, looking for her, for the horse. I don't see the horse and there are no barns on this property that I know of. I stop the car halfway down the drive.

She's not here. I can feel it. And the way she is with animals, now that he's hers, she'd never leave that horse behind.

I throw my arm around the passenger headrest, staring out the back windshield as I kick the car into reverse. Gravel kicks up from my tires as I tear down the driveway.

"Fuck!" I hit the brakes, hard, my head slamming forward. There in the rearview mirror is the horse, standing on the road just at the end of the driveway. My wife sits on top, one hand on her hip, the other holding the reins.

Shooting me death rays from her gorgeous gray-green eyes.

I cut the engine, flying from the car. "What the hell are you doing on the road? I told you to stay put."

"You also said you'd be here in fifteen minutes. It's only been ten. And my God, who drives like that? You almost hit my horse!" She pets his mane.

Her horse. She cares more for that beast than her own personal safety.

I plant myself in front of her. "Get down from there. Now. I want to talk to you. And do not bring up your brother. That conversation is over."

"I just went for a ride. I needed to clear my head. I won't say why." Her eyes are cutting.

"Don't."

"You were so fast. I thought I'd be back before you." She hops down from the horse.

She doesn't even have to hold the reins. That horse isn't going anywhere without her. He's as enamored of her as I am.

I catch the scent of smoke in the air and my stomach recoils.

"Don't you understand?" I rub a hand over the back of my neck, trying to keep calm, to be rational. I can't. "When I couldn't find you... when I saw the smoke...I thought you were dead."

Her voice is quiet. "I'm not her."

Her words hang in the air between us, heavy and sad.

"I know that," I say. "Don't you think I know that?"

She shakes her head, looking down. "I'm sorry. I didn't say that to be cruel. I'm sorry if it hurt you. I just mean... you can't worry over me like this. Just because something bad happened to her, it doesn't mean it will happen to me." Her gaze rises to find mine. "I'm not Emily. I'm Emilia."

I stand there and I just stare at her. My beautiful, brave, strong wife. I didn't see this coming. I didn't seek this. Hell, I didn't want this marriage. But it came all the same and it's the best damn thing that could have happened to me.

She's right.

She's not the little girl I lost. And even if I knew I would lose Emilia too, I couldn't live without her.

I'll take every day with Emilia that this world offers me.

"You're right," I say. "I'm sorry."

Her hand goes to her chest. "Is that... another apology? From Liam Bachman?"

"Yes. It turns out that my wife makes me a better man. I can apologize. Come here."

I hold my arms out and she falls into them. I lean into her hair, inhaling her warm scent. She feels like... home.

"As of today, I'm going to stop living in fear. I promise." I kiss the top of her head.

"Thank you." She looks up to me, searching for a kiss for her lips.

I brush my mouth over hers.

I run a finger along the back of her neck, making her shiver. "But that doesn't change the fact that I'm going to punish you right now."

21

E *milia*

WE'RE BACK IN THE ATTIC ROOM, MY HEART HAMMERING JUST AS HARD as the first time. We had a long discussion on the ride home about Antonio, and I'm coming to accept what happened. Liam, though, will not accept that I left and broke my promise to him, without punishing me. I stand shrinking back against one of the velvet sofas as he turns a copper crank in the wall, then smashes a large metal button.

The circle in the center of the floor turns; this time, a low, long, armless red leather bench rises from the floor.

Liam circles the bench, his steps as sleek as a panther's. "What do you think this is, my darling queen?"

My stomach flips. "I... don't know."

He steps to me, finding the zipper of my black workout jacket, fingers brushing my skin as he tugs it all the way down, the material parting. He pushes the jacket down my arms, letting it drop to the floor.

My breasts feel heavy, my nipples straining against the white tank I wear. He circles me, moving behind me, fingers digging into the elastic band at my waist. One smooth tug and he's got my pants and panties down to the floor.

The tank suddenly feels very sheer with my bottom half completely nude. He leaves it on. He drags his fingers down the backs of my arms.

"So beautiful. And all mine to do what I will."

Wish I had panties on right about now as arousal pools between the tops of my thighs.

He runs his hands down my sides, cupping my hips. He pulls me back into him, slides my hair from the back of my neck to over my shoulder, nipping kisses over the curve of my neck. His lips breathe hot words in my ear, sending a tremble through me. "Anything I want."

"Well, I don't know about anything..."

He takes my shoulder in his mouth, sucking and biting at it. He runs a hand down my ass, squeezing it till I gasp, shooting up on the balls of my bare feet. "Anything. Give me your consent. Ask me to punish you."

I know this is his way, how he resolves conflict between us. Instead of a fight, or him being angry at me, he wants to take me to his attic room and punish me. And it works for me. I want it this way. The mafia way? I don't know, but I consent.

"Punish me," I say. "Have your way with me."

"Thank you, I will."

Tickles of nervous energy trip down my spine; I know what he's thinking.

He wants to take me where he's never taken me before. It'll be part of my punishment. He loves to punish my ass. I'm no stranger to the gold plug now, but this will be the first time he's had me there with his cock.

He moves me to the bench. "Lay down with your elbows on the bench."

The bench is narrow. I try to get on it like a lady but there is no way to get on that bench other than to straddle the damn thing, legs wide apart, my feet pressing into the floor, my stomach flat against the bench. Elbows on the bench, I ball up my fists, resting my chin on them. It's narrow; barely wider than my body. He moves around me, brushing against me as he leans down, reaches under the bench, and pops out a leather pad on either side of me.

"For your knees," he says.

"Oh my God." I lift my right knee, settling it down on the padded knee rest. I do the same with the left. My inner thighs press against the edges of the bench as I straddle it. I'm... comfortable... for the most part. Other than the fact that my thighs are spread wide, my sex and ass fully on display from behind.

He leaves me lying there while he walks around the room. First, the music begins, those beautiful violins swelling, their music filling the air. The lights around the room dim as the chandelier lowers slowly, the fire-like flickering bulbs coming to life one at a time. He walks across the room, now in my line of vision.

He glides across the floor, his attention on the tools that hang from the wall. My throat feels weird, and I swallow back nerves, watching him choose. He walks by thin paddles, thick straps of leather, eventually walking his fingers up the dark blue wall to a long, thin gold stick, a doubled-over round of black leather attached to its top.

He takes it off the wall, his dark eyes meeting mine. He opens his palm, tapping the loop of leather against his hand. Each time the leather strikes his palm, I give a little jump.

"Stings," he says, a devilish grin spreading across his face.

I swallow, again. "Yes…"

He strides toward me, heavy shoes hitting the hardwood floor as he makes his way, tapping that thing the whole time.

My ass cheeks clench together in anticipation of the punishment to come. He stands over me. I wait for the spank, but instead, he lays the tool along my spine, leaving it resting on my back.

What's he doing?

He leaves me, the light whip sitting on my back. He goes to his drawers, pulling out something I've not seen before. It's a pink silicone toy, shaped like a thin, narrow scoop. It's a vibrator. It has to be.

I hide a groan as he comes up behind me. He lays the toy on my bare right ass cheek, grabbing my hips. "Lift." My knees press into the leather knee pads as I raise my ass in the air.

He turns the vibrator on, its soft hum tickling my nerves and my eardrums. He slips the toy between my legs.

"Oh. God." The soft vibrations buzz against my clit. His hand flattens against my lower back as he pushes me back down on my stomach against the bench.

A moan escapes me, my hips wiggling, to get closer to or away from the toy, I'm not sure. It's teasing me, giving me pleasure for a moment, then… gah… it stops. I whine, wanting more.

"I can see everything from back here." He pushes two fingers into my sex. "You're so wet. I can see how much your pussy wants me."

He thrusts his fingers inside me just as the vibrator comes back to life. The friction builds inside me, desire growing thick in my throat. "Ah... oh... my... God..."

"But it won't just be your pretty pussy getting my cock tonight." He pulls his fingers out of me, turning off the vibrator and sliding his slick fingertips up to my asshole. He circles my tight muscles, then pushes the tip of his finger into my ass. "I'll be taking this tight little ass too."

He fingers my ass as he turns the vibrator on again. The stimulation is too much, the humming vibration against my clit and my sex, while his finger teases my ass. Then he's gone and the vibrator stops.

He lifts the whip from my back. He drags the leather over my curves. "You have a perfect ass. You know that? Perfect for punishing."

He snaps the leather against my ass, making me jump against the bench. It stings, a bite of pain blooming over my skin. The vibrator comes on, pulsing against my sex.

I let out a low moan, leaning into the pleasure of the vibrator. Another stinging swat lands on my ass, just as the vibrator cuts off.

I need the damn vibrator to stay on. It's killing me, the way it's turning on and off like this. Just when I get the first hint of climax, the pleasure cuts off and I have to start over each time the vibrations come back.

I fight to speak. "This is torture."

"No, babygirl." He snaps the leather part of the whip against my ass again. "This isn't torture. This is punishment."

The vibrator kicks in, massaging my clit as he drags the leather loop up the insides of my thighs, over the slickness of my sex. He lifts it and to my shock, snaps it back down against my asshole.

"Ow!" I throw a look over my shoulder. "Seriously?"

"Watch the sass or I'll be putting a gag in that pretty mouth of yours."

My mouth snaps shut, my head looking straight forward once again.

"Let's have ourselves a little chat." As he speaks, he alternates spanking me with the leather each time the vibrator turns off. I'm panting, perspiration dotting under my arms as he works me over. "I don't ever want you to leave this house again without an escort. Is that understood?"

"Yes, sir." Oh my God, please let me come. "I totally understand. Can we, um..." I wiggle my hips against the onslaught of vibrations. "Move on now?"

"Naughty girl. So impatient. I think I want to spank this pretty little ass some more first. I like seeing the red welts pop up on your sweet curves."

He spanks me again. The pain bursts over my ass, the entirety of my curves hot and prickly from his toy. The vibrator comes on again and I'm whining, wanting it to stop, wanting everything to stop, or go forth, or... gah. Just something. I. Need. To. Come. "Please. Please."

He drags the leather loop over my ass. "Please, what, baby girl?"

"Please, turn off this toy and fuck me."

"I will. But I'm not done punishing you yet, you know that, right?" He taps the loop against my wet, throbbing entrance. He drags it up, snapping it against my asshole again. "Tell me how else I'm going to be punishing you tonight?"

"Ah..." Oh my God, don't make me say it out loud. But now the vibrations are back, and I can't take it anymore. He snaps the whip against my asshole again. A cloud of shame swirls around me as the words fall from my mouth. "You're going to fuck my ass."

"Yes, that's right. I'm going to take you here." Fingers circle my wet pussy, the slickness moving up to my ass as he pushes against the tight ring of muscles. "Then I'm going to shove my cock in this tight little hole and make you scream my name. Ask me for it."

"Please... fuck my... ass." God, can a girl die of shame?

"Good girl. Thank you for saying the pretty words I needed to hear." His hand dips between my legs, taking away the vibrator.

"Thank God." I take a deep breath, sinking into the bench. Relief runs through me, but only for a moment. I hear him unbuckle his belt, shoving his pants away. He moves in front of me, his cock standing hard and ready. He looks down at me, the head of his cock just past my lips. "Show me how sorry you are. Take my cock in your mouth and get it all wet for your tight little ass."

My chin rests on my fists and I open my mouth. He pushes the head of his cock inside, the slick drop of precum salty against my tongue. I wrap my mouth around his satiny skin.

"Good girl," he says, slipping a hand into the hair at the back of my neck. He guides my head forward, thrusting his cock deeper into my mouth till I'm choking on it, saliva slipping down my chin. He pulls back, leaving the head of his cock in my mouth as he leans down, kissing the top of my head. "Such a good girl."

He pulls it from my mouth. I quickly wipe my chin with the back of my hand. I watch with wide eyes as his cock, now shiny with my spit, leaves me as he walks behind me.

He thrusts two fingers inside me, making me gasp. My hands fall, grabbing the edges of the bench. He strokes my insides, bringing his open palm down against my ass, three times, hard and stinging as he fingers me. All the friction comes back, building, building.

"I'm going to come. Oh my God, I'm going to come."

"No, you're not. Not yet." He takes his fingers from me, slamming his cock into my pussy. My back arches, my fingers clawing at the leather. "You're not allowed to come till my cock is in your ass. Or we start this whole process over again. Learn to obey."

Oh, God. I can't. My sex tightens around him and I will the orgasm to go away, pushing it deep down inside. Please. God. Don't let me come.

He fucks my pussy, hard and fast, and all I can do is squeeze my eyes shut tight and pray I don't come. The friction builds in the walls of my sex and if he keeps going there's no way I can't not come.

He pulls his cock from me. I pant for breath, relieved I made it. My empty sex clenches, wanting more stimulation. I'm so close to the climax my body so desperately needs. The head of his cock presses against my ass. A deep breath shudders through me as he slams the full length of his cock into my ass. My muscles lock down onto him, the orgasm I've been begging for finally tearing through me.

A whining moan rises in my throat as his cock buries deep inside me. The feeling is strange, overwhelming, my ass full, my pussy clenching. Another orgasm wells in my core, wanting to be freed.

Just when I think I can't feel any fuller, he grabs my hips, pulling me back to him.

"Oh God." The orgasm tears through me, my entire body feeling like one muscle that's locked down on him. My ass muscles tighten, pulsing like they're milking his cock for his cum.

"Baby. My God, baby. Your ass feels so fucking good. You're so fucking tight." It finally comes, hot, filling my ass. It runs out, hot and wet down my thighs.

He collapses over me, licking and kissing a line across my lower back.

I can't breathe, can't think, perspiration rising from my hairline, my heart thumping against the bench.

The brush of his stubbled jaw, the heat of his tongue, his lips drawing the warming calm of the afterglow. I finally catch my breath, my eyes closing as I lay there, enjoying the closeness. He runs a hand over my hair, smoothing it back from my face. "So beautiful."

A smile slowly stretches over my lips, the cat that got the cream.

What he says next makes the smile turn to absolute sunbeams.

He pulls me up, helping me from the bench, turning me to face him. His dark eyes find mine, and what I see there melts me completely.

His voice is thick, full of emotion. "I love you, Emilia."

The words I've longed to hear. The words I've longed to say.

"I love you too."

We kiss, our mouths and our hearts locked into one another.

In love.

I'm living the happily ever after you only get in a romance novel. I think of my beloved books, hidden away. They gave me so much comfort when I didn't have the real thing. Now that I'm living the story with Liam, what happens to my books?

I think they've earned their places on the shelves.

22

L *iam*

"BABY, WE HAVE TO GO."

She doesn't even look up from her book. "One more chapter? Please."

"We have to leave." I go to her, taking the book from her hands. "You can read on the jet."

Her eyes go dreamy as she smiles, gazing around her just-finished library. "But just look around. How can I leave this place?"

The walls are a deep green, her mother's books neatly lined on the teakwood shelves. *All* of her mother's books, even the dog-eared romance paperbacks. She's curled up in one of the fuzzy cream-colored armchairs she and Charlie ordered, an empty teacup beside her.

"Don't you want to marry me all over again?" I brush my lips over hers. "This is the day you officially become a Bachman."

She looks away. "I'm nervous."

"There's nothing to be nervous about. You don't have to do anything. Just be there and say your vows. The Beauties take care of the rest."

"There's no secret stuff I have to do, or hazing, or rituals, or—"

I grab her hand in mine. "No. It's beautiful. You'll love it. I promise."

"Okay." She gives a little sigh. "I guess I can leave my library behind for a few days."

"And Journey and Mr. Patches and Banana Bread," I say, making it clear there are to be no furry stowaways on this trip.

She eyes me. "But Little Pet is coming. You promised."

"I know. He's already in his kennel."

She looks at me like I just said I had Marta fry up the damn dog for dinner.

"Kennel? Why is he in a kennel?" she asks.

"Last time he got sick on the plane. Remember?"

"He'll be fine," she says. "I promise. I won't feed him this time."

"You fed him on the plane?"

"What, am I supposed to eat prosciutto right in front of him and not share?" She changes the subject. She turns her pretty face over a tanned shoulder. "Let's go. You said it yourself, we need to leave."

"You're changing the subject."

"Liam. That doesn't sound like me at all." She sashays across the room, her blue dress fluttering behind her, a queen in her palace.

I smile, enamored by the confidence she's discovered since becoming my wife. She's dived into her sexuality, brimming with sensual energy in every move she makes.

How can it be that I've grown even more obsessed than when I first chased her down on the road that night? I follow her out.

The ride to New York is smooth. We dress for the ceremony, heading straight to the Village. Emilia could have had her pick of gowns, but she insisted on wearing the very same ivory one she wore at our short ceremony at the Parish.

To her disappointment, Little Pet stays behind in our honeymoon suite as we travel to the Village.

We reach the ground floor of the three-story brick building. We ride the elevator up three flights. The doors open, revealing the open-air, rooftop bar. Everyone is here for us, waiting with smiles on their faces. A few Beauties are already dabbing at tears glistening in the corners of their eyes.

The family all wears... *purple?* I gaze out over the crowd.

"What's going on?" I ask. "I've seen you wear that color gown before. But I've never seen everyone dressed in the same color at a ceremony before."

I look to Emilia as she whispers the word, "Emeria." Tears spring up in her eyes. "They wore my color."

"Emeria." It's a beautiful shade, one that looks stunning on her. Now, it makes me chuckle to see the men in Emeria tuxes, with their crisp white shirts and black bow ties beneath. The women each wear a gown with a different style and fit, little details making their dress stand out, but they are all the same shade of purple.

"I can't believe they did this. What a sweet gesture. I feel so welcomed."

Hundreds of white globe lights crisscross above us, dotting the dark sky. From their black cords hang lazy bows of wisteria, the flowers' soft scent filling the cool night air. An aisle has been made, leading from where we stand to a platform we'll use as an altar. Sitting on the ground in two lines are huge bouquets of David Austin roses filling wide glass vases, the same rose I handed her that night in the Parish.

A breeze blows softly, the scent of roses and wisteria brushing by with it.

I hook her arm in mine. "Ready?"

She smiles up at me. "Yes."

"I love you, Emilia." I hold her arm tighter in mine.

"I love you too, Liam," she says.

We make our way up the aisle to Rockland who stands on the platform, looking good in his Emeria tux. He greets us with a smile.

"Who gives this woman to be wed today?" he asks.

"I do," I say.

There's a wave of laughter in the crowd. Our little family joke. Unless your father is in the Brotherhood, he wouldn't be allowed here tonight, so all of us grooms give our brides away.

Rockland continues. "Welcome to all who have gathered here this day to share in this marriage ceremony of Liam Bachman and Emilia Accardi. These words spoken today are sacred and celebrate a lasting bond that already exists between Liam and Emilia, who have joined their hearts together and chosen to walk together on life's journey. Today, as Bachmans, we bear witness to the pledge of a sacred, eternal bond." Rockland's voice drops, his eyes going stoic. "One that may not be broken."

And it never will be.

"Those of us in attendance today are present to witness a statement of lasting love and commitment between Liam and Emilia. The ceremonial union of two people in marriage, in its primordial form, is as ancient as our very humanity and yet is still as fresh as each day's sunrise. The commitment of love between them is more than a declaration of love. It is a promise to remain loyal, faithful, and in service to one another until the day that death parts the two of them. All gathered are present at this ceremony to celebrate their marriage and to witness their vows of love to one another. Will all of you, gathered here to witness this union, do everything in your power to love and support this couple now and in the years ahead? If so, please respond, 'we will.'"

A resounding, "We will," rises from the crowd.

"And Liam and Emilia, have you come here today with the intention to be joined into the unique bond that is a Bachman marriage? Do you pledge to remain faithful, loyal, and to adhere to the ways of the Bachman family?"

I turn to Emilia. In unison, we say, "We do."

"Then let us witness the exchange of vows. Liam, please repeat after me. I, Liam, take you, Emilia, to be my wife; to have and to hold from this day forward; for better, for worse; for richer, for poorer; in sickness and in health; to love and to cherish; until we are parted by death."

I say the words, my heart welling in my chest.

"And now, Emilia, please repeat after me. I, Emilia, take you, Liam, to be my husband; to have and to hold from this day forward."

She holds my gaze, speaking calmly and clearly for everyone to hear. "I, Emilia, take you, Liam, to be my husband; to have and to hold from this day forward."

Rockland says, "I vow to accept your headship over our family. To obey your word. To accept your discipline."

She repeats Rockland's words. "I vow to accept your headship over our family. To obey your word. To accept your discipline."

Rockland continues. "For better, for worse; for richer, for poorer; in sickness and in health; to love and to cherish; until we are parted by death."

Emilia finishes her vows, smiling at me.

We exchange new rings. Matching platinum bands from Bachman's Jeweler, the date we met engraved inside of them. My fingers linger on hers when I slip the band over her finger. "I love you."

Now for the final piece in the ceremony. The last threshold to cross.

The lights cut.

Emilia looks to me with a nervous grin. I squeeze her hand, the feel of her new band under my fingers. "It's alright. You'll see."

EMILIA

MY STOMACH FALLS INTO MY RED-BOTTOMED SHOES.

With one last reassuring smile, Liam leaves my side.

I stand there, alone, in the center of the dark aisle and swallow, hard, waiting. For what, I have no idea.

Then, in the dark, the light of a single candle burns.

It moves toward me.

Liam is holding a white pillar candle in one hand, a red Bachman's box in the other.

He reaches me. The candlelight dances across his handsome face. His eyes are soft with emotion.

He passes the candle to Rockland and opens the box.

In it sits a necklace with a charm, small diamonds forming the shape of a tiny sword. I've seen the other women wear them before but hadn't thought much of it.

Liam speaks, his gaze fixed on mine. "All Bachman women own this necklace. It's a symbol of our creed, the way we live our lives, the eternal care of a man for a woman. For as long as the stars have lit the sky, men have cared for and loved the women they have pledged their lives to. And women have loved and obeyed those men, accepting them as the headship of their family. Choosing to give the gift of their submission to these men—men who would *lay down their lives for the ones they love.* The sword is our symbol—the length we are willing to go to, the sacrifice we would willingly make; to kill for you, to die for you."

Liam hands Rockland the empty box and steps around me. His body brushes up against my back. He brings the chain around my neck. The little sword rests on my chest. His fingers are at the back of my neck, clasping the delicate necklace in place. His hands rest on my shoulders. "Emilia, I freely give you this symbol, and pledge my very life to you. Do you accept?"

"I do."

My fingers go to the charm. It's beautiful. "Thank you." My lips meet his and I kiss him deeply, feeling my love for him all the way down to my toes.

When my eyes open, I find each Bachman holding an unlit candle. Liam turns to Rockland, taking back his lit candle and lighting Rockland's with it. The gesture continues down the line until there are hundreds of twinkling lights dotting the rooftop.

Rockland holds his candle high as he speaks. "Fire, also as timeless as the Earth, symbolizes the Bachman family's pledge to one another. To guide, care for, and protect one another above all others. Bachmans, do you accept the union of Emilia and Liam?"

"*We do,*" the hushed voices reply.

A shiver runs down my spine.

"And Bachmans, do you pledge to care for and protect Emilia and Liam as you would your own blood?" he asks.

"*We do.*"

"And how long will you hold these two in your care?"

"*Forever.*"

He turns to me. "Welcome to the Bachman family, Emilia."

The quiet reverence of the evening is broken with rowdy cheers.

Rockland comes to me, kissing both my cheeks.

Then, it's Liam's turn to kiss me. He kisses me deeply, with passion, leaving me grinning and lightheaded. He releases me and I'm passed from person to person. Hugs, kisses, words of congratulations wash over me, welcoming me to the family.

When I'm passed back up to the altar, Liam is standing on the platform, a microphone in hand. Music fills the air. Charlie stands beside me. A whispered, "I can't believe it," leaves her lips as she stares at Liam.

I grab her hand. "What's he doing?"

"He's going to sing," she says.

"What's he going to sing for?" I whisper back.

Charlie gives me a heady grin. "For you."

My voice squeaks. "For me?"

Then both our attentions turn to Liam as his voice fills the room, sultry and smooth and oh-so-sexy.

Every woman in the place has their eyes on me wishing it was their man on that stage singing to her.

Every man in the place has their eyes on Liam wishing they sounded like that when they open their mouths to sing.

I feel embarrassed by the attention, overwhelmed by the gesture, and excited and happy, but everything melts away when his eyes meet mine, singing words of love and longing to me and it's just so out of character for him to do this, I feel my heart welling with even more love for him.

Afterward, we sit at rectangular tables covered in white linen, dining on the rooftop. My mother's roses sit in a vase on the table. Everyone from The Villa, our Bachman home in Italy, sits at our table here in the Village tonight.

I catch the soft scent of the roses. I've got my mother in me. That's what Antonio said. And he never says something he doesn't mean. I sit at my place at the head of the table, my spine straight, shoulders back, a genuine smile on my face, shining over all the members of our family.

The long table holds half a dozen brothers, me, and Liam at the other head, looking incredibly handsome as always, the candlelight illuminating his bronze skin and dark, glittering eyes. A canopy of fresh flowers hangs, suspended by thin black netting, creating the illusion of thousands of roses floating in the air over our heads.

Charlie sits beside me, sipping chardonnay from her glass. My best female friend in the world. I invited Marta to dine with us, but she declined, preferring to oversee the staff as they serve us hot dishes of buttery seafood and seasoned vegetables.

I sit and look over all the gifts that have been given to me: friends, family, love. I know I'm strong enough to wear my crown as queen.

I, too, can soothe my husband with a touch on his arm. Roses bloom in the garden and I'm the one who's tended to them. My home is filled with light and love.

I have my mother in me.

And my king by my side.

Liam stands from his seat, proposing a toast. The grin he gives me melts my heart all the way down into the red soles of my Louboutins.

He raises his glass in the air. "To my wife. All hail the queen."

"All hail the queen!" the table choruses, clinking crystal glasses together, their shining eyes smiling upon me.

It was a hard-fought battle. There were two clear winners.

Long live the king and queen.

THE END

EPILOGUE

C *annon*

WHEN PEOPLE HEAR THE TERM "KINK CLUB," THEIR MIND DRIFTS TO somewhere dark and underground, a palace of shame to be hidden from the world.

Not my club.

Hidden from the world, yes. It takes a full year to be vetted to join unless you have an in with me and my family. But dark and dingy and shameful?

Hell no.

I'm proud of my place. I built it from the ground up and now socialites from all over the world fly in to experience a night at my club. It's a place so beautiful, you could bring your mother. Well, maybe don't bring your mother. Might be awkward as hell for you. But you could take her. It's that nice.

We bring the heat to Italy.

Fire is not your typical night club, not only for what we do inside, but for where it is. When I first had the idea for the club, I found a luxurious historic estate at the top of a mountain, a stone wall with iron gates protecting the property. When I first pulled up to the stone mansion, surrounded by lush olive groves, I had one thought...

Fucking sexy.

I love sex. To me, to live you need water, air, food, and fucking. Fucking comes in all forms, and I say it's the same as work, do what you love.

No judgment. If you're playing with a consenting adult, have at it.

A member of my undercover security hovers in the corner of my eye, dressed in plainclothes, a black suit, the top three buttons of his collar undone. As soon as Grace is out of earshot, he leans down, his voice low in my ear. "We have an issue."

"You know how much I hate to hear you say that." Of course there're kinks when running a kink club, but I prefer my nights to run smoothly. "What do you have for me."

"A girl."

"A girl?" I glance around the room. We're surrounded by dozens of beautiful women, their clothing ranging from none, to barely there lingerie, to evening gowns. "What girl?"

"About three minutes ago, a young girl dressed in street clothes came to the door with a guest pass key. We'd never seen her before and she wasn't with a client so we kept an eye on her. She went straight to the elevators and removed a package about the size and shape of a brick, wrapped in brown paper, from inside her sweatshirt. She stood there for a moment, then hid the package behind the pots of one of our Monstera plants."

She'd better not have hurt my Monstera. That thing cost a fortune. I run a hand over my brow. "Did you retrieve the package?"

"The Head of State is there, lingering, waiting on someone. I have someone posted by the elevator bay, eyes on that plant, ready to retrieve the parcel as soon as Marcus' attention is elsewhere."

"Good. Where is the girl now?"

His finger goes to his ear. He presses the button on the hidden device, then waits, his lips pursing as he listens.

He looks at me. "Headed this way."

"Let me know when you have the package."

"Yes, sir." He nods. "And the girl?"

A curvy little brunette comes dashing down the hall. Heading right toward me. Something about her makes me speak before he answers me, saying, "Actually, I'll take care of the girl."

"Yes, sir." He takes his leave.

The girl spots me behind the bar and rushes over.

"Is there a manager here? I really need to apply for a job." Her heart-shaped face turns to me, hazel eyes filled with innocence begging me. Her short bubblegum pink nails tap the bar as she shifts her weight on white sneakers. "Like, yesterday."

Who is she, asking me for a manager? Everyone that steps foot through that door knows who I am, and that I own this club.

She doesn't look a day over twenty. And her clothing—jeans and a loose sweatshirt—tells me she doesn't understand the first thing about this club or what we do here. My job applicants wear their sexiest, very best couture knockoffs to apply here, knowing if I accept them, they'll soon be able to afford the real thing.

"You want a job?" I ask.

"Yes." She nods.

"Here?" I ask.

She flashes me a nervous look. "Yes, sir."

I laugh, wiping down the bar. "You don't know the first thing about what we do here. I think you'd better head back to town. I think there's a children's clothing boutique that might be hiring."

She slaps a palm on the table, pleading eyes grabbing mine. "I need a job. Here." The desperation in her voice makes me stop.

I drop the rag, washing my hands in the bar sink. I dry them on a fresh towel. "Come. Sit. Tell me why you're really here. Who told you about this place?"

Her eyes dart right, then left. "I, um, don't know. Just a friend, you know. They said the pay was good."

"What's their name?" I know every single employee by face and name. I do all the hiring, male and female dancers, bartenders, scene masters. I handpicked each person on my diverse staff. They all have three things in common. They're hard workers, want to improve their station in life, and they all have an almost inhuman ability to be discreet.

Discretion is everything in this business.

The housewife of a prominent mobster should be free to come to my club and be a pretty little kitty for the night, complete with a tail and velvet ears—with her husband's permission, of course—without fear that she'll later bump into someone in town who will taunt her about her kink.

"Who sent you?" I ask again.

She shakes her head, looking away. "Oh, they said not to say."

She's a terrible liar. I get the feeling she's not very practiced at it.

"Is that so?" I ask.

She nods. "Yes."

"Can I tell you what I think?" I ask.

"I guess you're going to."

"Yes, I am." I move in closer. "I think you're a little girl who's somehow gotten herself into some trouble and you heard whispers of this place and how we protect our own. You want a job here, as a hideout, a way to protect yourself."

The color drains from her face as I speak.

Telling me I'm dead right.

I slide a finger under her chin, tilting her eyes up to meet mine. "Answer me. Is that why you're here?"

She shakes her head, preparing to tell another lie. "No. I... um... I..." Her face falls, her lips trembling as her eyes fill with tears. "Yes. Okay? I'm in trouble."

I stare at her, debating whether to kick her out or ask her further questions. My instincts are good. My intuition is part of what makes me such a valuable player in our powerful mafia family. I follow my gut. And right now, my gut is telling me to show this curvy brunette the door sending this admittedly gorgeous damsel in distress on her way.

But my cock is stirring as she sinks pearly white teeth into that full bottom lip of hers. And *he* says...

Game on.

SNEAK PEEK MAFIA FIRE
BY SHANNA HANDEL

Mafia Fire: A Dark Mafia Romance

The little beauty came to my kink club, Fire.

Brought something she never should have touched.

I punished her for it and sent her on her way.

But I can't stop thinking of her.

How innocent yet sensual she is...

I have to be the first to have her.

She's in trouble with more men than me.

They don't just want to punish her.

They want to own her.

I can't let them have her.

She's gone from someone I can't stop thinking of...

To something I have to possess.

She's burning me up. Turning me to ash.

My little mafia fire.

Chapter One

Kylie

THEY'RE NEVER GOING TO STOP TILL THEY GET WHAT THEY WANT FROM me. And it's something I'm never going to give. I peel the note off my front door and read it again before I go inside.

Your family owes us. You know what we want.

I MAKE MY WAY TO OUR LITTLE BLUE AND WHITE KITCHEN. IT'S STILL spotless from when I cleaned it this morning, the electric teakettle sitting in the same spot I put it after I wiped the counters down. Grandma hasn't gotten out of bed yet.

My fingers shake as I tear the paper into pieces, tossing them into the trash. I've got to find a way to fix this. I wrap the end of a long strand of my dark hair around my finger, twisting and pulling it tight, a nervous habit I've tried to break but which lately seems to be happening more often.

I stare out the window to our patch of shaggy grass in the backyard. It needs cutting but the mower broke. Another thing that will have to go untended. At least the wildflowers from the seeds my mom spread years ago came up this summer right on cue.

I need money. A lot of it. Fast.

If I can't get the money, then I need to find protection somehow.

And if that fails...

I push the thought from my mind. I can't bear the idea of what I'll have to do. This is exactly why I took that job this morning. Great pay and, hopefully, the Accardis will become attached to me enough to protect me.

My grandmother calls to me from her bed. "*Tesoro,* sweetheart, is that you?"

"Yes. I just got home." I kick my boots off by the door, padding down the hall in my sock feet. I peek in her open door. She's buried in the piles of quilts I tucked around her. Does she look even more frail than when I left this morning? "Would you like some tea?"

She shakes her head. "Pane, vino e zucchero, please."

Her favorite snack, bread covered in wine and dipped in sugar. I should make her eat some meat or cheese with it, but I haven't been to the store today. "Bread and wine it is."

"Thank you, Kylie."

"Only the best for you, Nonna."

In the kitchen, I cut a slice of bread, putting it on my mother's beloved gold-rimmed china, little pink roses dancing along the plate's edge. A cherished possession she brought back from the

States with her. Along with her hazel eyes, short stature and round hips, the dishes are something I inherited from her.

I sprinkle the bread with tons of sugar, the way Nonna likes it, and pour wine on top until the sugar is colored. I bring it to her on a tray with a fork, knife, linen napkin, and a jar filled with a bunch of wildflowers I picked from the backyard.

Time to tell Nonna the good news.

I set the tray down on the bed beside her, helping her to sit up to eat. I sit down next to her.

She takes a delicate bite of the bread. "Perfect. Thank you."

"Nonna, I got a job today."

Her brow furrows. "Don't you already have a job?"

"Yes, but working at the drug store doesn't pay as well as this new job." I finger the soft petals of an orange wild lily. My stomach flips with nerves, wondering how much to tell her. I don't want her to worry.

"But it's a good job, no? Your mother and I got by on what we made there. We're doing just fine."

"Yes. You're right. It's a good job." My legacy: the third Barone woman to work at the corner pharmacy in town, walking distance from our tiny yellow cottage. "But I found a better one."

"Where is this wonderful new job?" She runs the tines of her fork around the plate, collecting sugar crystals on her bread.

"It's a housekeeper job. For a very wealthy family."

"For who?" She eyes me, still not convinced I should quit the pharmacy.

"The Accardis."

My grandmother's brow furrows. "Hmm... the Accardis. I thought they were broke. Spent up all their mom's money after she passed. Beautiful Bella. Those boys were lost after she passed."

A silence stretches between us as we think of my mother. She went to college in New York then stayed, building a fancy life for herself as a designer. She even had her own high-rise apartment in Manhattan. Then she got pregnant, moved back to Italy to our small town, and took up right back where she left off. Living here in our little yellow house, working at the pharmacy down the road.

She died giving birth to me.

My throat feels tight, thinking of her. I clear it. "Yes. But they've come into a new fortune. Apparently, they've got some new business deal. Pretty lucrative, from what I've heard."

Nonna makes the sound she makes when she disapproves of something. "Humph." She shakes her head. "And that generous dowry they got when they arranged for their daughter to marry one of those Bachman boys."

"Only my grandmother has the balls to call the men of the Bachman Brotherhood 'boys,'" I laugh. "And I don't care where the Accardis get their money, as long as some of it gets into our pockets."

I'm desperate.

Nonna eyes me. "Well, you've got balls too and you know who you get them from. Now, are you going to tell me why you need more money? Do we have some bills I don't know about?"

I shake my head. "Nothing to worry about. Just wanting, you know, some nicer things for us." I kiss her cheek, clearing the tray from her lap.

I rinse the wine from my mother's china.

How do I tell Nonna that my uncle, her beloved son, has stolen from the wrong men? That while she thinks her baby boy, Marco, now a middle-aged man, is off traveling the world, really he's passed out behind the train tracks, out of his mind from the drugs he bought from the Meralo clan.

Bought being an exaggeration.

The Meralos gave my uncle Marco an advance on his drugs, then a second, then a third.

He owes them a lot of money. Money they've come to me to collect. I can't tell my grandmother the truth, it would break her heart. So, I let her think Marco is still traveling the world.

And I hope to God she doesn't find one of the pretty little notes the Meralos have been leaving on our front door before I have time to tear it up and toss it out.

The morning brings gloom and rain, the perfect backdrop for walking up the gravel drive to the Accardi's haunted mansion. Black shutters hang over peeling green paint. The overgrown brush has recently been cleared away from the house, but the gardens are still in turmoil, weeds choking rosebushes as they struggle to survive.

My fingers grip the leather strap of my purse as I stand before the massive, black front doors, deep rectangles in the wood. I take a closer look at the carvings in the door handle.

The carvings are angels.

Angels... they have to be a good sign, right? Nonna says I'm always trying to find the good in the bad, the hope in the dark. I run a finger over the knob, tracing the wings of a tiny, long-haired angel. "You're my good luck."

The door swings open. I step back, snapping my hand away. An angry-looking man about my age stands in the doorway, his dark hair hanging over one of his bright green eyes.

"You're late."

"Am I?" I glance down at the watch on my wrist, a delicate oval on a thin, tan leather band. Another item of my mother's. It's nine a.m. "I'm right on time—"

My words cut off as a glint of silver catches my eye. He looks right at me, dragging the sharp end of a metal hook down the frame of the door.

The hook is the man's hand.

I've heard rumors of Antonio Accardi. How he taunted his sister, Emilia, when she lived here, touching her where he shouldn't, and of how her new husband, Liam Bachman, cut off Antonio's hand in revenge.

I guess the rumors are true.

"Antonio?" I ask. I hold out my hand to shake his. "Pleasure to meet you. I'm Kylie. I did a phone interview with your father? He hired me, told me to be here at nine, and here I am." I repeat, "Right on time."

He looks at my hand and gives a grunt. I pull it away.

"Kylie?" he says. "What kind of name is that? American?"

I shrug. "My mom lived in the States for ten years. She gave it to me."

He eyes me. "Your mom is dead."

Wow. Blunt much? "Yeah. I heard something about that."

"Mine too. I guess we have that in common. That, and we both hate the Meralos. You hate them." A nasty grin curls at his lips. "Don't you?"

I hold back, giving a question as an answer. "Heard something about that too. But what did you hear?"

His green eyes study my face. "Heard they got your uncle hooked on some nasty shit. Then stuck you with the bill."

I think of the notes. One every afternoon when I get home from the pharmacy for two weeks now, making demands of me.

I nod. "Yep. That's about right."

"Guess you're hoping for some protection along with that fat paycheck. Aren't you?"

Ice trips down my spine as he exposes my truth. My tongue feels tied.

"Well, am I calling it like it is?" He stares at me.

My answer is a whisper. "Yes."

He gives a nod.

"Maybe we can help each other out." He opens the door with his good hand. "Come on in, Cinderella."

I push past his dark ego, entering the dimly lit home. The place must have been gorgeous back in the days Bella Accardi's money and elegant touch graced it with their presence.

Now, it's filled with cobwebs and dust and grime. My little neat freak heart bangs against my ribcage. I love to make things beautiful.

Time to get to work.

Antonio shows me where the cleaning supplies are, a cupboard just as dusty and neglected as the rest of the house. Then he leaves me to clean his house and wonder what he means by *helping each other out.*

I know by the cunning look in his green eyes it won't be long before I find out.

Printed in Great Britain
by Amazon